Blood Empire

Book Three of the Blood Match Series

Melinda Call

Blood Empire, Book Three of the Blood Match Series

Copyright © 2025 by Melinda Call

First edition

ISBN: 979-8-9883767-7-4

Cover art by Megan at CryoMerch[1].com

Editing by Brandi at My Notes in the Margins[2]

---

1. https://cryomerch.com/

2. https://www.mynotesinthemargins.com/

Table of Contents

Copyright Page 1

Acknowledgements 5

Chapter One...6

Chapter Two...15

Chapter Three 24

Chapter Four 32

Chapter Five 37

Chapter Six 40

Chapter Seven 50

Chapter Eight...59

Chapter Nine..64

Chapter Ten..70

Chapter Eleven...79

Chapter Twelve...87

Chapter Thirteen 94

Chapter Fourteen 101

Chapter Fifteen 111

Chapter Sixteen 120

Chapter Seventeen 127

Chapter Eighteen... 140

Chapter Nineteen... 147

Chapter Twenty 155

Chapter Twenty-One 167

Chapter Twenty-Two... 175

Chapter Twenty-Three 183

Epilogue – Three Years Later 190

About the Author.. 194

Other Books by Melinda Call.. 195

Acknowledgements

This book is dedicated to my daughter, Megan. She has been deeply involved in this series from its inception. We've spent countless hours brainstorming transitions and plot, disagreeing about how certain characters look, and giggling hysterically at my random misuse of words and phrases. *Packing into the horses* might still be her favorite. She's saved me from giving away too much too quickly and from choosing formulaic and ultimately wrong endings for each of the three books in this series. Basically, Megan made this series and me better in the process. Thank you for being my alpha and beta reader and bringing the characters and covers to life. This series wouldn't have been possible without you.

• • • •

My editor, Brandi from My Notes in the Margins[1], has once again knocked it out of the park with her in depth review of this book. Her love of the characters and series comes through in her thoughtful notes. Thank you for pushing through the rollercoaster that was this novel. While this book may not have ended how she imagined, the story is not over and I'm hopeful that she will get the happily ever after she was hoping for.

• • • •

Megan does more than keep me on my toes and help me build worlds and characters to share with you. She creates all kinds of art. If you'd like to see more of her work, it can be found at CryoMerch.com[2].

---

1. https://www.mynotesinthemargins.com/

2. https://cryomerch.com/

Chapter One

My feet slapped against the treadmill as the bass exploded in my headphones, followed by screaming guitars. I closed my eyes and found the rhythm. The vanilla-lavender scented candles helped relax my tired mind. *Thanks, Eve.*

This was my sanctuary. The one place I could pretend to have my own life, a life I chose, the life I actually wanted. Where I could run off the tension and focus on breathing rather than what I've become. Rather than having the expectations and responsibilities that were literally thrown at me on New Year's Eve.

The song's tempo shifted and my feet stuttered. Not a good combination on the high-speed setting. I hopped onto the sides instead of falling on my face and opened my eyes. Beyond the floor to ceiling windows, trees were visible in the fading evening light. Trees, trees, and more trees. This was my home now.

I powered down the equipment and patted myself off with the little towel someone had left for me. My ponytail was stuck to my back. *Gross.* When I turned, I nearly fell.

"Sorry," a little voice squeaked.

"Dammit, Dona. Stop sneaking up on me!" I yelled, pulling out my earbuds.

She shifted her weight between her feet and looked down in submission. Blonde curls fell about her round face as she folded in on herself in apology. She'd spent decades with Seraphine so she was understandably traumatized. Working together had been a lesson in patience. Both of us had a mountain of issues we were working through.

When I didn't threaten her life or something equally as horrible, she lifted her eyes and gave me a sheepish grin. "I did remember to knock this time."

I wiped the towel over my face to hide my exasperated expression before asking, "What can I do for you?"

Dona held up a tablet and squinted through her large round glasses. "You have a ten o'clock with Cassie at Gambini's. Do you want to take Rowan or Steve?"

I put my head back, biting back a scream, and let out my breath slowly. "Neither. Neither would be great. I'd just like to have dinner with my friend."

Dona frowned at her tablet again but didn't answer so I continued. "Cassie's been in security for years. I'm pretty sure she'll be better at protecting me than either Rowan or Steve."

"But that's not how..."

I walked toward her and put my hands on her shoulders. "Dona, things are different now. We can bend the rules a little considering I'm supposed to be the one making them."

Rowan decided at this moment to make an appearance. "As Steward, I'm inclined to agree with Dona but as the cheeky bugger I am, I think you can have one night alone. Besides, I've already made plans and Steve is still useless in a crowd. You'd be babysitting him with so many humans around."

"Thank you, Rowan. I think." I shook my head at both of them. "Can you guys hit the road? I need to get ready for my girly date."

Dona nodded and left the room. Rowan clasped his hands behind his back and waited. I was standing next to the free weights and at that moment wanted to throw an eighty-five right at his head. He'd been constantly underfoot for weeks. I needed a break.

"Yes?" I finally asked, hoping I didn't sound as annoyed as I was.

"Victor will be back tomorrow from his Council appointment."

I glanced at my watch to confirm the date. Victor's return had been looming but I'd been so busy, the months had evaporated. I had even scheduled my dinner with Cassie as a last-minute distraction.

"Thanks for the reminder. Now, if you don't mind..." I flicked my fingers toward the door in a shooing motion.

"You still haven't finalized his living arrangements." Rowan let his hands drop to his sides.

Yeah. That. So much for a relaxing evening. All of the freaking reborn immortals bound to me now lived *with* me. Or maybe I should say, I was stuck living with them. I missed being a spinster in my tiny cottage. Just another part of my life that had been ripped away. At least I had a few rooms on the upper floor that were all mine, at least while the sun was up.

"Could we, and hear me out on this... drop him into a volcano?" I suggested.

"You had the chance to break your binding and you chose to keep him. These are the consequences."

I let out another breath. "No good deed goes unpunished and all that jazz. The lower floors are still being renovated, correct?"

Rowan nodded but clearly caught my line of thinking. "I'll contact Eve to see if she can host Victor a bit longer."

"Thanks, Rowan." I gave him a genuine smile. While he was a pain in my ass, he had also saved it more times than I could count. "What are these plans you have for tonight?"

A mischievous grin spread across his face. "It's Wednesday. You know Wednesday is Bingo night at the Community Center."

"Rowan, you are a cheeky bugger." I laughed then added seriously, "Be good."

He nodded but didn't answer. I hadn't worded it as a demand so he'd have to use his own judgment. Lord, help us. I hadn't made any demands since that night I'd told Victor to open the blinds to full sun because I honestly didn't think it would work. The thought made my stomach clench. I never wanted to repeat that experience.

The shower made me feel like a human again but when I went to the sad collection of clothing in my closet, looking for my favorite shirt. I wanted to strangle my sister. She hadn't lost her entire wardrobe in a house fire, yet she still felt the need to pilfer my meager selection.

So far, I'd refused to use any of the Council's money on myself so my pathetic savings had gone into replacing the personal items I'd lost. The good news was I should be getting a sizable check from my insurance company since the arson claim had finally been approved. Thank God, Seraphine's people left my car alone.

I wrapped myself in my fluffy robe, *thanks again, Eve*, and stomped toward Acacia's room. The house was still quiet as the sun had set less than an hour ago. I knew my lazy sister would still be in bed. She'd taken a semester off to deal with her rebirth, which had been up and down from the start. We were six months in now and I was ready for her to do something other than sleep and draw.

I didn't bother knocking and just walked in and flipped on the light.

"AH!" Acacia screamed and smashed her pillow over her head.

I opened the closet and started flipping through the hangers. Everything was black or gray, with splashes of neon popped in occasionally. How did she ever find anything? The shirt in question was not in the closet so I started opening dresser drawers.

"What are you looking for?" Acacia asked.

I turned around and the little shit was wearing it! It was rumpled from sleep and appeared to have a red stain by the collar. I wanted to scream. One thing. Could I just have one thing today?

"Never mind." I took a step to leave. "I'm going to Gambini's with Cassie. Rowan is going to be out so unless Eve is coming here it looks like another solo night in for you."

She grumbled unintelligibly. Her newborn stage was something the Immortal Council had been very clear on. She was basically on probation, not trusted to *not* go on a full murderous rampage so her outings around humans were very limited and overly supervised. That thought took me back to her first "meal" after her rebirth. It's amazing the Council didn't lock me up like Seraphine.

"I'm out in half an hour. I'll enjoy a couple slices of mushroom and prosciutto for you."

"You are so mean." She tossed her pillow at me.

"Stop stealing my clothes and maybe I'll be nicer. See you later, brat."

As I slowly cruised the Mustang down the long winding drive, I chastised myself. The Immortal Council had given me this house and the land so that I could take care of my clan. They had given me money, more than I was comfortable thinking about, because I'd hit the genetic lottery in their eyes. I was an ungrateful bitch because I'd throw it all away to be a normal, boring human with a normal, boring human life.

While I was surrounded by people constantly, I'd never felt so alone or so *other*. Seraphine had been filling her reborn with lies about how the immortal world actually worked and who controlled it. She hadn't actually killed off all the living immortals in the US, more like she paid them off to stay hidden and not create new reborn. That murderous psychopath had killed several but not nearly as many as she let on.

In truth, she was just a spoiled brat who had been left unattended too long. Her father had been the head of the Immortal Council at the time and ignored her transgressions since they occasionally helped him get or stay in power. Luckily for me, she had pushed too far. I owed him my life, as well as Acacia, Rowan, and Victor's.

That was another thing I would give anything to walk away from. Victor. Having him follow me around like a lovesick puppy was one thing but the way he looked at me now that I was a living immortal was too much. Pedestal living was not for me. I was going to drink a lot tonight.

The new house was about twenty minutes north of downtown. Winters were a pain in the ass but it was gorgeous and the distance between homes kept the rumor mill low. Not many people in this part of the country had a half dozen non-relatives living with them, unless it was a cult. That thought made me laugh. The Cult of Arabella's Undead Misfits. How did I get so lucky?

I missed my chance to park on the street and had to circle the block. A black SUV followed me around the block. I couldn't see the driver, but I had a hunch. The parking spot was still open but I drove a block up and circled back again. The SUV mimicked me. I kept going and turned into a vacant lot, pulling all the way in the back and got out.

The SUV pulled in then stopped when the driver saw me standing next to the car. I motioned for them to keep coming forward. There was a moment of hesitation then the SUV pulled up and stopped. The headlights blinded me.

The door opened and Dona's blonde head peeked around the door. Yes, I was going to drink a lot tonight. I grabbed my purse out of my car, locked it, then went around to the passenger door of the SUV.

"I'm sorry-" Dona started.

I held up my hand. "Looks like you just volunteered to be my DD. Find a spot to park. I guess you're my impromptu plus one."

. . . .

THE RESTAURANT WAS not busy on the late weeknight, and they held bar hours so we didn't have to rush through our meal. Cassie was on her phone when we joined her at one of the high tables. Dona had to jump to get into her seat, which was impressive in her tight pencil skirt.

"Bye, babe. See you tomorrow night." Cassie finished her call then hopped down to give me a hug.

"Sounds like things are still going well with Dr. Blackwood?" I asked.

"Yeah, Stan's the best. He's working a double but had a minute to chat," Cassie answered then looked across the table at Dona. "Hi, I'm Cassie."

Dona stared at Cassie's hand for a moment then took it. "I'm Dona, Arabella's personal assistant."

"Nope. Not tonight. Tonight, you are just plain old Dona. What do you want to drink?" I handed her a drink menu then picked up the food menu.

Cassie giggled at our interaction. I'd only seen my friend twice since my return. Once at the hospital and once when I needed help shopping but due to budget constraints, didn't call Eve. Both times Rowan had been with me. The thought of the hospital visit made me frown. That was not what I wanted to think about tonight.

"What are you getting, Cas?"

"I ordered the spicy artichoke dip to share, chicken pesto flatbread, and Cuervo Gold shots all around." She turned to Dona. "You should try the peach lemonade martini. It's to die for."

Dona squinted at the menu so I just had to ask, "Dona, I know you don't need glasses. Why do you still wear them?"

She adjusted them and looked at me while squaring her shoulders. "They are befitting of my station."

Our waitress appeared at that moment with the dip, shots, and to take the rest of our order. Cassie gave her shot to Dona and ordered another. The delicious burn helped ease my tense shoulders.

"Befitting of your station? What is this, the nineteen-fifties?" Cassie asked. "Whoever told you that was trying to hide how pretty you are."

Dona looked down and if she could have, I imagine she would have blushed. "Thanks, but I'm not really that pretty."

"Who told you that?" I asked and she shrugged.

"Well, those guys over there have been staring at the both of you since you walked in so clearly you are not a hideous hag that needs to hide behind glasses," Cassie said then gave the aforementioned guys a dark look to make it clear we weren't interested.

I turned in my seat to see who she was talking about. There were two guys a few tables over. One was a ridiculously tall African American man, the other your average hipster, maybe Latino. Neither were hard on the eyes but yeah, this was girls' night. We'd hook Dona up another time. I, on the other hand, had sworn off men for the foreseeable future.

Cassie changed the subject. "Geo asked me to say hello. He misses you."

"I only caused him trouble. But yeah, I miss him too—and working. I really miss working. Any chance I could request work clearance, Dona?" She reached into her bag for that damned tablet but I put my hand on her arm. "In your opinion. I don't need to hear the statute word for word."

"You already work for the Council and our job is to keep you out of harm's way. Your old profession literally puts you there." She adjusted her glasses again then set them on the table. "But I know how it feels to be forced to do things you don't want. I'll see if we can find an exception. Just don't tell Rowan."

I clapped my hands together. "There you go! I knew there was a rebellious side to you, girl."

The night was pretty relaxed once we broke that ice. After stuffing ourselves and taking way too many shots, we had Dona drive us to Cassie's condo. While she mostly lived at Stan's place these days, they kept the condo as a place to crash after late shifts and the convenience of being downtown. I keep waiting for her to show me a giant engagement ring but they were doing things their way, on their own timeline.

I'd convinced our waitress to sell us a bottle of dessert wine to go. We turned on a movie about gladiators with scantily clad men that Dona watched with enough intensity to crack Cassie and me up several times. We kept reminding her it was fiction, not a documentary.

Dona got a call around two AM and excused herself. Probably Rowan. I sure didn't want to talk to him. I'd turned my cell off at the restaurant. Dona could run interference and was happy to do so. Tonight was for me, everything else could wait.

Cassie leaned over and in a quiet voice asked, "Have you heard from Tom?"

I finished my wine before I answered. "He's still on tour."

"That doesn't really answer the question."

I sighed. "I was the one who suggested we take a break, Cas. I'm not really the woman he proposed to anymore. Plus, there's the other thing. Somehow, both our lives took a sharp turn in opposite directions. I'm just not sure where we go from here."

"I still can't believe he has a kid." She hesitated then changed the subject when she saw my expression. "This is girls' night. Let's just enjoy the eye candy on the screen and worry about real life another day."

"Thanks, Cas."

At some point, we decided to give Dona a makeover. Despite being about the same height, none of Cassie's clothes were going to fit as they couldn't have been more opposite in shape. Cassie was sporty and lean compared to Dona's very curvy stature. After some time with a straightening iron and make up, I barely recognized her. Whoever told her she wasn't pretty was clearly blind, or just an evil, jealous bitch.

I snapped a photo on my phone of the three of us. One of my eyes was partially closed but I couldn't get them to take another as they were too busy laughing at me. Why did I always look like I was having a stroke or about to sneeze in group pictures?

When we got home just before sunrise, I regretted all the alcohol. There were a lot of stairs between me and my bed. I looked longingly at the couch but with a sigh I climbed the stairs to my rooms. When I lay down, the ceiling spun a bit but I smiled. I hadn't had that much fun in a long time.

Chapter Two

"You're touching me," I mumbled and rolled away, pulling the covers over my head.

I knew it was Victor from the cologne. Plus no one else would be sitting on my bed, brushing my hair from my face. While my reborn liked to pop in unexpectedly, we'd reached an agreement about personal space while I was sleeping. His rich laugh filled the room and my stomach clenched but not entirely because of my hangover. Why did I think that much wine was a good idea?

"That rule still stands?"

"Pretty much plan on that one forever," I snuggled farther under my warm covers.

He cleared his throat and stood. "We had a meeting at eleven. It's twelve thirty. I was just making sure you were still alive."

I let out a breath and peeled my eyeballs open. Pale light from the bedside table glowed through my blanket. My mouth felt full of cotton and my head was pounding. I needed a gallon of water and more sleep.

"Talk to Dona. She'll reschedule." I was still hiding and hoped he'd leave.

It had been six months since he walked out of Seraphine's mansion and out of my life. At the time, I fought against his punishment—having just officially accepted him and the others into my clan. Not to mention he had been trying to save my life just moments before. The Council meant to sentence him for a mistake he didn't make or even know about. A lot had happened since then.

Rowan kept me updated on Victor's activities by the request of the Council so at least I knew he wasn't dead permanently this time. The exact punishment was still unknown to me but he was back, which meant time served or something. He'd sent me a letter, clearly written under duress, but it told me things I wasn't ready to hear from anyone, especially from someone who had no right saying such things. Now, he was back and I had no idea what to do with him.

I peeked out from under the covers to find him still standing next to my bed. "Dude, at least give me ten minutes to get dressed and brush my teeth."

He chuckled as he left the room, closing the door silently behind him. I rubbed the palms of my hands against my eyes and felt the grit of the mascara I forgot I had been wearing last night. My hands were now covered in black smears.

Carefully, I got out of bed and headed to the bathroom. What I saw in the mirror made me cringe. Not the smeared makeup, which was quite impressive, but what was around my neck gave me pause. When the hell had I put that on? I didn't even remember where I'd put it once I got to the new house. To be honest, I didn't remember much after my climb to my room last night either. My subconscious knew Victor was coming home today. That was the only reason I would have put it on, right? All I could hope was that he hadn't seen it.

I laid the pink diamond and black pearl necklace on the vanity and turned on the shower. Ten minutes was not going to be enough but he could wait. The glass of water did nothing for my thirst so I scrubbed my teeth to try to remove the sweaters. After my shower, I needed food. Something fried and terrible for me.

My cell was ringing when I stepped out of the shower. Again, I didn't remember turning it back on before I crashed. What other bad decisions had I made? The screen showed a picture of me and Tom. My hand hovered over the phone unsure whether to answer or not. The image disappeared as the call ended.

I scooped up the phone and opened my messages. Oh no. I had drunk texted Tom. I opened the text message as the phone beeped indicating a voicemail. *Miss yu. Call ne when you cannn.*

Well, it could have been so much worse than mild spelling errors. At least he had called back. We'd had a few awkward conversations while he was on the road but I didn't really know what to say. He mostly talked about the cities he'd visited and his son. I didn't know who I was anymore, let alone how I was going to have anything that resembled a normal relationship. Today sucked. For now, the voicemail could wait.

I quickly dried my hair with a towel and pulled on comfortable sweatpants and V-neck t-shirt. My bedroom was quiet when I emerged. I seriously considered locking the door and hiding the rest of the night but I was really hungry.

I'd made it halfway to the kitchen when I smelled bacon. Someone loved me! My smile fell when I saw who was in front of the range. I grabbed an overripe banana from the fruit bowl and the orange juice from the fridge. The first bite nearly came back up. I did not want fruit. I wanted a bacon and fried egg sandwich made by anyone but him.

"Dona told me you went out with Cassie last night and needed someone to drive you home. I thought maybe you'd like some breakfast." His eyes dipped to my neckline briefly. Yep, he'd seen the necklace.

Another gag and I spit the banana into the trash. Never look a gift breakfast in the mouth, no matter who makes it. I opened the cabinet above the fridge and grabbed the vodka. The shower was not enough. Only hair of the dog was going to help bring me back to the land of the living.

He set a plate in front of me at the breakfast bar. "There is a way to make that hangover go away almost immediately."

I poured a good amount of vodka into my orange juice and took a long drink. "I made the bad decisions, now I have to live with the consequences."

He frowned and I realized my statement could have a double meaning. Considering how uncomfortable he made me, returning the favor felt good. I took a bite of my sandwich and closed my eyes, suppressing a moan. If Victor had one redeeming factor, it was his cooking. Maybe I could assign him that job.

Rowan had stressed that everyone in the clan needed to have purpose, or more specifically, a job. Pierre hadn't been joking when he said a living immortal couldn't navigate this world alone. As much as I'd like to go back to work for Geo, I had no free time. Besides trying to learn all of the Council's laws and rules, which at this point I was convinced were never ending, I was also learning about what I was.

Victor had stepped out of my field of vision while I enjoyed my sandwich but I could still hear him moving around. The click of a briefcase and papers shuffling led me to believe he had actual business to discuss at this meeting. I finished a second large glass of vodka infused orange juice before turning to the dining table.

My nemesis was sitting with his back to the dark windows. Three neatly stacked piles of papers rested in front of him. He fidgeted with a pen. Clearly, he was uncomfortable with what he'd brought to this meeting. I pulled out the chair opposite and sat. This could be interesting.

He motioned toward the first stack of papers. "The Immortal Council requires someone to serve as legal counsel for your clan. I will have completed the necessary steps so I can practice law in Montana by the end of the month. My standard retainer fee is indicated here." He split the stack at the yellow sticky tab. "If you'd prefer someone else, the Council provided a list of approved alternatives."

I leaned forward and pulled the top stack toward me. There was a lot of legal jargon but basically Victor would represent me and the rest of my clan members on all legal matters both Council and otherwise. His retainer fee seemed a bit steep, but the Council was covering that, not me. It made perfect sense so I easily found the correct places to sign. They were marked with colored tabs and in triplicate. It was like he actually did this for a living.

Victor let out a breath like he was surprised I signed without a fuss. I decided more orange juice was in order so I grabbed the rest of the bottle and sat back down. Victor organized the first stack into separate folders and moved the second stack closer to me.

"As your attorney, I would recommend you have a professional manage your money. Traditionally, that role is completed by the clan Steward but Rowan doesn't really have that kind of background." He smiled almost to himself. "I happen to know a very talented accountant who is used to managing this type of sizable estate."

I glanced at the paperwork and smiled too. If anyone would give me honest advice, it would be Lucian River. Dona had been paying the utilities and ordering groceries since we arrived but the Council kept her busy as well. When it came to tax season, I would have needed someone anyway.

This stack was easy to review and sign as well. Maybe this meeting would be pretty painless, minus my still pounding head. I needed to add aspirin to the next grocery list. Victor shifted in his chair and restacked the last set twice before pushing them my way.

I glanced at the first sentence and pushed them back. "No."

Victor folded his hands in front of him and sat back. "This is not something I wanted but the Council is pushing for this one."

"I'd rather have Acacia take this role. She's family after all." I crossed my arms, not breaking eye contact.

"She's barely eighteen and still considered transitioning. Power of Attorney isn't something she can handle at the moment."

"And I'm really not comfortable with you making decisions for me, especially if I am incapacitated. If not Acacia, how about Rowan? He's taken the role of Steward a little too well. He clearly has my best interest at heart and at this point, has given me no reason not to trust him."

"His little coup nearly got you kill..." Victor started then looked over my shoulder.

Rowan sauntered into the room and slapped Victor on the back then mimicked rubbing his shoulders. "I've missed you, Mate. What are we talking about?"

"Rowan, how would you feel about holding power of attorney for the clan?" I asked.

He held his hands up in surrender. "No can do, Ara. My role as Steward can contradict long term decisions. Plus, I'm not really one for paperwork. That seems more like Victor's cup of tea. Hmm, tea..."

I seethed as they ganged up on me. "How long do I have to make this decision?"

"If you suggest Steve, I will find you mentally incompetent," Rowan said as he filled the kettle with water. "He's happy running and patrolling the grounds but he's more a doer than a thinker."

"You don't have a lot of options at this point. We can reassess once your clan grows." Victor held the pen out to me, but I didn't move.

I kept my arms crossed and raised my eyebrows. "How long?"

He placed the pen on the top sheet and sat back. "The paperwork will be filed with the Council's clerk in two weeks."

I pushed to my feet. "Looks like I have some time then."

Crashing near the front door drew my attention. I hurried that way, grateful for the distraction. Rowan was speaking to Victor in a hushed but intense tone but I didn't care. No wonder he left that stack to the end. Victor would never be making decisions for me again. There had to be another option.

Eve and Acacia were adding boxes to a large pile already in the entryway. "What's up, girls?"

Eve bounced over and smothered me with a hug. "Thank you for letting me stay here while they deal with the mold issue at my condo."

I looked over her shoulder at my sister who wouldn't make eye contact with me. Apparently, she'd overlooked telling me that her girlfriend was moving in. Honestly, I wouldn't mind having Eve around. It could get pretty boring during the day. Then the full consequences of her words hit me.

"Eve, this is a lot of stuff. How long were you planning on staying?"

She stepped back and looked sad. "Um, I don't know yet. They have to completely remove all the drywall. The contractor didn't use any vapor barrier so the entire complex is unsafe. I thought Acacia told you."

I pasted a smile on my face. "Don't worry about it. Clearly, we have plenty of space. Let's put you next to Acacia."

"Eve!" Rowan enveloped her in a hug and rocked her side to side. "Do you need help with the rest?"

"We've got it." Acacia took Eve's hand and pulled her back outside.

I punched Rowan in the arm. "You knew about this? Why didn't you tell me yesterday when I suggested Victor stay with Eve?"

He rubbed his arm. "Because you needed a night without stress. Victor's here to help. I'll make sure he doesn't overstep."

"Rowan, he was sitting on my bed when I woke up. I'd call that overstepping, wouldn't you?"

He cringed. "I'll talk to him."

The girls appeared with Eve's giant beanbag chair so I helped them move it downstairs into an empty room. We spent the rest of the night moving Eve's stuff into two rooms. There was no way everything was going to fit into one. It looked like she had moved almost everything here. I wondered if her plan was to stay long term.

After a few minutes of thinking it through, I decided it didn't matter if she moved in permanently. I had more than enough space and no intention of adding to the clan anytime soon. The upside meant I wouldn't have to wrestle that damn beanbag chair back up two flights of stairs.

Victor must have moved in somewhere too but I didn't go looking, I was just glad he didn't try to continue our earlier conversation. We finished the night by watching a movie in the screening room. I enjoyed doing something normal with two of my favorite girls.

The Council had planned on repurposing the screening room and gun range into living space. I quickly put the kibosh on that. If this was going to be my house, I wanted those things. Movies had always been my go-to for downtime or to destress. Cassie had been helping me with my marksmanship, but I still had a long way to go. Having a range at the house would definitely speed up the process.

Once the girls had gone to bed and the house was quiet, I stepped out onto the porch and watched the sun come up. The pale yellows and pinks filtered through the trees giving everything a soft glow. My cell phone felt heavy in my pocket. I opened the voicemails and pressed play.

"Hey. I couldn't sleep after the show so I thought I'd call but didn't think about the time. I'm sure you're asleep. I'll try again soon. Love you."

I listened twice then watched the colors brighten against the trees. Besides the gym, this was the only time I had to myself. The screen door slid open and I amended my last thought.

"Arabella?" Eve sat on the edge of the chair next to me. "I'm sorry we ambushed you. Acacia said it was okay."

I tucked my phone back into my pocket. "It's okay, Eve. It'll be nice having you here. I miss hanging out and it can get pretty lonely during the day."

Eve sat back and we enjoyed the sounds of nature for a few minutes. She kept wiggling and taking in a breath as if to speak. I yawned and moved to get up.

"Can I talk to you for a second?" Eve's words were rushed.

I sat back down and prepared for the worst. Eve rarely struggled with speaking her mind, unless it was something that would upset someone. In that case, she would tie herself in knots until she over-thought every possible scenario. Apparently, this was her only option and she knew I wasn't going to like it.

She lifted her chin and looked me in the eyes. "I want to start the process of becoming a reborn."

I closed my eyes and let out a breath, deflating a little. That was not where I thought she was heading by moving in here, but it made sense. She clearly was in love with my sister and her brother was also a reborn.

"Eve, you don't know what you're asking."

"I do! I've talked to Acacia, Victor, and Rowan. I want to do this." She took a deep breath. "I'm ready to do this."

"Even though you're ready, I'm not sure I am," I confessed.

"But you turned Acacia."

"That was different. She was going to die if I didn't."

"And I might die driving to school tomorrow. You don't know. I don't want to die, Arabella. I know I can do so much good if you'll just..."

"Eve, I didn't say no. I'm just saying, not yet." She gave me a sad smile so I continued. "How about you and I sneak out of here? I suddenly have a craving for pancakes."

Chapter Three

To say Rowan was unhappy was a gross understatement. He even suggested moving Eve into a hotel, since sneaking out of the house must have been her idea. If he only knew how wrong he was. We'd grabbed breakfast then went shopping. I now had a few more clothing options and new slippers. Eve ended up with an armload of new books.

"Arabella, you are too important for us to not know where you are," he explained.

"More important than caramel pecan pancakes?" I tried to joke but he didn't even crack a smile. "I'm sorry, okay? Yesterday was not awesome. I needed a minute to be normal."

He hesitated before continuing. "I understand, but you've got to meet me halfway on this."

"Fine. Next time, I'll leave a note," I promised and tried not to grin at his stern expression warning me there better not be a next time.

As if to make sure I wasn't getting too haughty, he added, "I know it's not what you want to hear but you've finalized your binding with everyone but Victor."

We were in the kitchen and I was attempting to enjoy some coffee. His comment made it turn sour in my mouth. I had kind of forgotten about that. Since I hadn't turned anyone but Acacia there was a blood sharing ritual that had to be performed to solidify the clan binding. It was awkward but tolerable with Rowan and Dona. Steve was... Well, he was Steve.

"The Council has given you an extension due to his punishment but you're running out of time. He's already on thin ice. Rogue status..."

"I know. I know. It's just different with Victor." I rubbed my face with my hands. "With you guys, it's just business. You're all like family now. With him..."

Rowan nodded in understanding. "Why don't you just talk to him about it?"

"Why don't you just add that to the list of things that are never going to happen. And for the record, I'm still voting for that volcano."

Rowan shook his head but chuckled under his breath. I chugged the rest of my coffee, which was still too hot. Stop making terrible decisions!

"Dona said she had some scheduling fun to review so I guess it's back to work for me." I rinsed my mug then pulled my hair into a ponytail. "Can you ask Steve to cut back the trees on the main drive? I don't really want to scratch my car every time I leave."

"If he doesn't, would it keep you from leaving?"

"Not likely," I mumbled under my breath as I left the room

Dona was in her office. Actually, it was my office but I gave it to her. What did I need an office for? The view was one of the best in the house. The rich mahogany desk and matching built-in bookcases spanned the room. She looked like a little girl sitting at the huge thing.

I plopped down on the tan leather couch and put a brightly colored throw pillow over my face. Dona moved around the desk and sat in one of the matching chairs near me. Her nails tapped on her ever-present tablet.

"Victor will be accompanying you to the Immortal Council when you update them on your clan's progress. I've moved a few things around. If we book your flight for Monday night, that will give you a day before you meet with them. Does that work?"

I pressed the pillow against my face and wished to suffocate. After a few moments, I sat up and sighed in defeat. "Sure. Tell me more good news."

Dona adjusted those damn glasses and scrolled up on her tablet. "Um, I need to book you a room at a Council approved hotel. Should I get one room or two?"

"Any chance we could stay in different hotels?" I asked and her mouth dropped open. "It was a joke, Dona. Two rooms, obviously."

"Did you still want to have dinner with your parents this Sunday?"

"You know what, let's move that to Saturday."

She made the update. "I'll give your mom a call—"

I quickly interrupted, "No need, I've got this one."

Mom was brought up to speed with both Acacia's and my new life. Well, as much as she needed to know. She was still mad at me for canceling the wedding so she'd been distant over the last few months. My dad had been suspiciously absent whenever I'd scheduled a dinner at my parents' house so I hadn't been able to corner him to pass on Pierre's message or ask him a few questions. I needed at least a few answers before I was back under the Council's scrutiny.

Dona and I went over the rest of my schedule for the week then launched into this week's lesson: Immortal Council history. I tried to listen, but my mind and heart were not in it. It wasn't long before I found myself daydreaming and eventually just asleep.

I dreamed about the last day Tom was in the hospital. I dreamt about it a lot but I could never change the ending, not in the dream or real life.

"I'm here to see Tomas River." A female voice pulled me from my magazine.

"Ma'am. I'm sorry but only immediate family is allowed in this area." the nurse explained.

I was hanging out in the waiting room while Tom got his last breathing treatment. He was set to go home tomorrow if his oxygen level stayed where it was. Well, Eve's house since I hadn't told him about my change of living arrangements yet. I had planned on telling him everything tonight so he could decide how we moved forward from here.

I was alone except for a little boy playing with the train set and watching cartoons in the corner. We had restricted visitors once the media got wind that Tom was in the hospital and which one. Several fans had sent flowers then they just started showing up.

"You don't understand. He needs to see his son."

I stood and peeked out the door. The woman was facing away from me. Her strawberry blonde curls pulled at a distant memory. I turned back to the boy. He too had his back turned to me and time slowed down as I moved toward him.

My heart broke when I finally saw his face. He looked just like the painting in Lucian's office. The woman at the nurse's station must be....

"My name is Rachel Olson. Just tell him, please," the woman begged.

This was the push I'd needed. I walked up behind her and gently laid my hand on her shoulder. She turned in a huff, probably expecting someone to force her to leave. Victor had been right. She and I did look alike, kind of like a prettier cousin or older sister. My voice stalled for a second, so I turned to the nurse.

"It's okay. I'll tell him they're here." I turned back to Rachel. "Give me a minute, okay?"

She hiked her bag back onto her shoulder and nodded. I could tell she was sizing me up. There was no doubt she noticed the resemblance too.

A nurse was wrapping up the breathing equipment when I stopped in Tom's doorway. His color was coming back but he'd lost a lot of weight. I'd danced around what had happened in California because he needed to get better. My time to procrastinate was over.

"He's all yours," the nurse said as she rolled the equipment past me.

"Thanks." I closed the door and pulled a chair next to Tom's bed.

"I recognize that look. I'm not going to like what you're about to say. Did they decide to keep me another day or something?" He tried to laugh but it just made him start coughing again.

I waited until he stopped and realized I'd been twirling my engagement ring around my finger. I slipped it off and set it gently on the bedside table.

27

"Tom, I'm sorry for everything. Actually no, not everything. We had something amazing."

"Had?"

I stood and lifted my shirt, exposing where my scar should have been. "I'm not what you think I am. I wish more than anything that I was but I'm not, and I don't know if I can be anymore."

Tom scooted closer to me and reached out. "I don't understand. Where's your scar?"

"I heard what you said to Victor about the reborn." I felt a tear slide down my cheek and angrily wiped it away. I had practiced this speech a hundred times and needed to be strong.

"But you didn't go through with it. You're still my Arabella."

"I'm not that kind of monster. I'm the kind that makes them." The words came out in a rushed sob. His expression broke me and tears rolled down my cheeks. "I can never be what you want, Tom. I can't give you the life you want but apparently there is someone who can. You need time to think about what that means. I have all the time in the world so when you've made your decision, let me know."

Tom picked up the ring and shook his head. "I don't understand what you're saying. You are everything I've ever wanted."

I walked to the door and motioned at Rachel. "Not everything."

I jerked awake when someone touched my arm. Dona was standing over me. I must have slid down the couch when I fell asleep. My cheeks felt wet and her concerned look told me I was crying in my sleep again. I thought I was done with that but apparently hadn't stopped the embarrassing habit.

I sat up and wiped my eyes. "I need to go."

Dona didn't try to stop me. When I stepped into the main hallway that would take me to my rooms, Victor stood at the other end. Instead of hiding in my room, I turned and walked outside. Right now, I didn't have the strength to talk to anyone, let alone him.

I WANDERED AROUND THE grounds for a few minutes taking deep cleansing breaths to chase away the memories. As I neared the drive, I heard a strange whacking sound. Welcoming the distraction, I jogged up the driveway toward it.

An overly muscled bald man wearing a loose tank and sweatpants was hacking the encroaching limbs with a machete. I slapped my palm to my forehead. Of course that was how Steve would trim the trees and bushes. At least Rowan had relayed my request.

"Hey Steve. Have you ever heard of an electric chainsaw or hedge trimmer?" I asked when he finally noticed me.

He bowed slightly and I frowned at his formality. "Yes, of course but I find this works better. Working with my hands keeps me closer to nature. Plus, it's a great workout."

"You don't have to work out to keep in shape, Steve. You're exactly how you were when you died."

He looked down at his hands then grinned at me. "Then it makes me feel like I'm alive. Want to try?"

I took the proffered blade and slashed at a bush. The edge sliced through the limb cleanly. It actually did feel pretty good. We took turns working on one side then the other for about an hour. Four large piles of branches were stacked neatly on the side of the drive when we finished. Someone, probably Steve, would move them to one of the small sheds so they could be used for fireplace kindling in the Fall.

While we walked back to the house, I asked him a question that had been bothering me for a while. "Steve, how old are you?"

He gazed ahead and squared his shoulders. "I was alive when Rome was at its pinnacle. My father was a poor man and sold me to work at the colosseum as a boy. The gladiators teased me for my skinny stature and stutter, so I spent all my free time getting strong. Once I was the man you see now, my master put me in the games. I beat many gladiators and became a champion, but my stutter kept me from gaining favor with the royals. All but one."

"Let me guess. He was a living immortal who promised you fortune and fame?" I asked.

Steve shook his head. "He promised me vengeance on those who tortured me as a child, for those who looked down on me still. I had as many whores, sorry... I had as many lovers as I wanted and none of them laughed at me. I was a true champion."

"What happened?"

Steve rubbed his neck. "My master started starving me of blood. Longer and longer until I would black out in a blood rage. He told me it made me a better fighter. During one of these episodes, I killed the emperor's niece. I was banished from my clan and given to another.

"I was passed from clan to clan whenever it suited them. I was with Pierre for centuries but he gave me to Seraphine shortly after her death. He told me to protect her as she built her clan. Finally, I had a purpose and, in the beginning, she was kind. She swore to take care of me and I promised to protect her."

"She didn't keep her word, did she?"

Steve shook his head. "She put me back into gladiator games but as a fool, not a fighter. Everyone laughed. I felt like the skinny kid all over again. That's why I don't like crowds."

I stopped and gave him a hug, which he awkwardly accepted. "I won't ever laugh at you. But hang on, you said you were teased about a stutter. Your speech is perfect."

At my words, he returned the hug, popping my back in the process. "I had a good teacher. I believe you've met Joseph? He spent many hours helping me. He's a good man."

"Steve, are you okay that I decided we should all call you that? I was pretty upset at the time and didn't really think about your feelings. Your real name is just so dang long. What was it again?"

He laughed and nodded. "Septimius Tervis Cassius Evoulus. But I like Steve. People don't have names that tell their family's story anymore. Steve is a good strong name. Strong, like me."

I gave his enormous bicep a squeeze. "There's no one stronger. Thanks for joining my clan. You make it better."

"No, Arabella. You make all of us a little better."

Chapter Four

My eyes ached from staring at the computer screen. I'd had five video meetings in a row with either councilmembers or other living immortals wanting to welcome me. I wished they'd all just leave me alone. If I had to explain why I hadn't known about the Council until last year one more time, I was going to start making up ridiculous, dramatic stories instead of the truth. Maybe the rumor mill would move from interest to horror and they'd stop calling me. My eyes turned upward and I silently prayed for a storm to take out the internet.

Everyone had been so nice to Victor since his return and he'd been, for lack of a better term, different. I kept watching him, expecting the old Victor to appear any second but so far nothing. He'd even stopped staring at me like I might somehow disappear in a puff of smoke if he looked away. I still tensed when I caught a whiff of his cologne or stepped into a room where he was, but I seemed to be the only one with a problem.

I could hear laughing when I left the office. On the back of the main floor was what I referred to as the Game Room. The large space held pool and air hockey tables, darts, and a pinball machine, which I sucked at. Steve had all the high scores. A table and chairs sat in the corner with a chess board at the ready. A couple of overstuffed chocolate-colored chairs sat by the bay windows. The room had also been outfitted with light blocking covers so it could be used anytime. So far, I was the only one who'd enjoyed it while the sun was up.

I'd never learned to play chess but it looked like Eve was showing Acacia. By the number of pieces in front of her, it looked like she was catching on quick too. She'd always been a fast learner. Checkers was more my speed.

"Steve, it's not how hard you throw," Dona explained as she flicked her wrist, landing the dart in the center of the board, "it's all about control."

He nodded then proceeded to bury a dart into the wall next to the board. I bit my lip to keep from laughing. Rowan and Victor were playing pool. I hovered just outside the room and watched my clan of misfits.

Rowan cursed as he lost another game. "Looks like I owe you a beer, Mate." He noticed me standing in the door and added, "I'll get us both one."

He leaned in close when he walked by. "Be nice."

I rolled my eyes and took the pool cue from him then spoke to my nemesis. "Rack 'em up. Let's see how you do against someone who actually knows how to play."

Victor hesitated and, for a moment, I thought he was going to refuse. Finally, he grabbed the rack and set up a new game. I tossed the cue ball in the air and slowly walked around the table.

The sharp crack when I broke was louder than I had anticipated and I realized the other conversations in the room had stopped. Tension between Victor and me was enough that people had started walking on eggshells when we were in the same room together. That needed to stop. My goal was to make this a home for the entire clan, even me. Balls flew around the table, two striped ones disappeared into opposite pockets.

"Not a bad start." He added chalk to the end of his cue and passed a little too close behind me considering the size of the room.

Eve started talking a bit too loudly about chess stats. The thunk of darts started up again. Tension dispelled. *Team effort*, I thought.

Victor made a tricky bank shot and for a moment I considered a wager. I'd let him win this round then I'd bet something painful. Even though a truce was on my mind, I was in a bad mood and wanted to take it out on someone. This game would give me time to think about how to do that.

Rowan returned with two beers and a ginger ale. I popped the top and took a long satisfying swig then rolled the cool can against my neck. Victor completely missed his shot. Ah, the façade was starting to slip. I thought about Rowan's suggestion to be nice but fuck it. This "new Victor" was just another act and the sooner we got it over with the sooner we could start moving forward.

I bumped Victor with my hip as I leaned in for my next shot. He took a long draw from his beer and stepped well out of my way. Rowan had joined Dona and Steve at darts explaining a new game they could play. Eve sounded cross and I knew Acacia was beating her mercilessly.

"So Vic, what are your plans now that you're back?" I was across the table from him as I lined up my shot.

He coughed and raised his gaze from the low neckline of my tank top back to my eyes. "Once I file the paperwork for the Council, I'll have some time on my hands. Do you have any suggestions?"

My cue skipped along the felt and the ball spun wildly, knocking in a solid. I was supposed to be distracting him not the other way around. He'd let his persuasion dip into his words. I'd become very sensitive to it after a bit of coaching from my sister. The words from his letter filtered through my mind. He had told me exactly what he wanted to do should he find his way back to me. Not really a conversation for the entire clan to hear.

"That is completely unfair!" Eve shouted and stomped out of the room. Acacia scrambled after her.

"My sister is not known for being a good sport. She likes to win." Victor finished his turn and I realized our game was over too. I'd lost.

I took another drink of my ginger ale and considered leaving. This was a dangerous line I was walking but so was he. Neither of us liked to lose either.

"Best two out of three?" I asked.

He smiled and set up another game. Rowan, Dona, and Steve disappeared sometime during the third game. Apparently, Rowan decided I wasn't going to kill Victor and left us to ourselves. I'd

34

destroyed him in round two but this one was close. Time to up my psych game.

"What do I get if I win?" Victor asked as another ball disappeared.

His gaze was intense, insinuating, and I frowned. It looked like I wasn't the only one playing mind games. No one was around to prove his behavior change. I took my turn before answering.

"In your dreams, pal. But it doesn't matter because I'm two shots away from wiping the floor with you."

And I was. The 8-ball disappeared and I did a little victory dance. Victor hung both our sticks on the wall then turned back to face me.

"Alright, Winner, what do you want?" Victor asked as he crossed his arms over his chest.

I paused, noticing the quiet house as the sun was about to come up. "I want you to answer a question. Honestly."

"I'll do my best."

"Why did you write that letter?"

His expression darkened and he glanced away, a sure sign he was lying. "I thought I was going to die, permanently this time."

"So, you didn't mean it."

He turned his eyes back to me, dropped his arms, and held my stare. "I meant every word, but..."

"But what?" I asked when he hesitated.

He shook his head and turned to leave. "It doesn't matter. Everything has changed."

I grabbed his shoulder and roughly turned him back to face me. "Why? Because it's not a game anymore? I'm not some prize you can win?"

He grabbed my upper arms and forced me to take a step back. "You were never a game to me."

"Then what?" I spat, mad at everyone and everything.

He was an easy target for my anger, but his next question threw me. "Why did you break off your engagement to Tom?"

"None of your damn business." I stepped around him. He was not going to derail this conversation.

"Please, Arabella. I need to know."

The sadness in his voice broke me but I kept my back turned and lowered my head as I answered. "Because I'm not that person anymore. Tom deserves better than what I've become."

"What's wrong with what you've become? Arabella, he is an idiot for even letting you try to walk away. If you had been mine, I would have moved heaven and earth to make you see how special you are, how much you are loved."

"No!" I turned around and shoved him hard in the chest, forcing him to take a step back. "*You* don't get to say that. Not you!"

"Why? Because it's the truth?" he snapped back.

"Because I need someone to hate more than I hate myself!" I gasped as the words left my mouth. The truth like a punch to my gut, stealing my breath.

He didn't try to stop me when I walked away this time. Words have power when spoken out loud. You can't take them back. They leave scars deeper than any blade. I was a monster and wasn't ready for anyone to see me as anything else.

Chapter Five

The air was hazy with smoke as I pulled behind my dad's truck, effectively blocking it in the driveway. When I opened the car door, the scent of wildfires and heat slapped me in the face. It was much hotter in the valley than at my house.

I knocked lightly and attempted to push the front door open but to my surprise, it was locked. My parents never locked the door during the day. I lifted my hand to knock louder then waited until my mom's face peeked around the living room curtain.

"Hi honey, I thought you were coming for dinner tomorrow night." Mom pulled me in for a hug then asked, "Where's your sister?"

Her shaky tone told me why the door was locked. She was afraid of what happened, of how she'd lost her daughters. If only I could help her understand the threat was gone. And lastly, I hoped, more than anything, that she wasn't afraid of us.

I held on a moment longer, savoring the connection of the hug. "It's only seven, Mom. She'll be asleep for at least another three hours. She did want me to tell you hi."

"Oh, that's right." She gave me a sad smile. "Your dad is grilling steaks out back. Go keep him company and I'll start reheating some leftover chicken."

"Sorry I mixed up my days. They all seem to run together these days."

I followed her inside, grabbed two beers, then headed out toward the grill. Dad was poking the meat to test for doneness when I approached. He closed the lid and I popped the top on one of the beers.

"Hey dad, thought you might like some company." I handed him the open beer and opened the other for myself, tucking the caps and church key in my back pocket. "And we need to talk."

He took the bottle, looked toward the house, and asked, "How's your sister?"

"Driving me crazy, like always. She's not here, but you know that."
I took another sip and attempted to put my words in order. "Why
exactly would the leader of the Immortal Council want to send his
regards to you?"

"Maybe he's polite?"

"Really, Dad? How long have you known him?"

His shoulders dropped a bit and he took a long drink, looking
chagrined. "They showed up at the house a few days after you were
born. At first, I thought it was some sort of scam. The stories they
told were outrageous but they insisted on regular visits and support.
For years, I tried to ignore them but like clockwork they would show
up exactly one year later. When you turned twelve, instead of
councilmembers showing up, a box was delivered."

"Twelve? That's when I had my party in the park downtown. You
were on a job and showed up just in time for cake."

He nodded. "I hid the box and didn't open it for a full year. When I
did, I knew the life they were offering wasn't the life you wanted. And,
as your dad, I needed to protect you."

I pulled him in for a hug. He held me tight and for a moment, I was
the person he wanted me to be. Understanding washed over me and
with it a sense of peace instead of anger over being kept in the dark for
so long. Even so, I felt like I needed whatever was in that box if I was to
move forward with the life I was now attempting to navigate.

"Where's the box now?"

"In the crawl space."

"Let's go have dinner and I'll take it with me when I leave. Thanks
for taking care of me, Dad. I wish you had told me. Maybe things would
have been different? Better? I don't know."

"Arabella, honey, if there is one thing I know, you will not be told
what to do. If I'd given you that at twelve or thirteen, you would have
gone to the Council and told them where to shove it."

I clinked bottles with him. "You know what? You're absolutely right. Maybe I still will."

As we walked back to the house, I wished that was an option. The faces of Dona, Steve, Rowan, and Acacia flickered through my mind. I'd never abandon them. They were my family now. I needed to stop fighting this and start owning it.

Dinner was the most normal thing I'd done in a while. We talked about Mom's real estate business and the crazy things Dad had pulled out of toilets recently. Toddlers flushed the most interesting things, making me glad my 'kids' were grown adults. Rowan might be an exception but he was manageable most days.

I gently deflected any topics I knew would upset my mom, especially anything about Tom or my current living situation. Neither of them had been to the house yet. I just hadn't figured out how to soften the blow that I wasn't really who they thought anymore. It was easier to pretend this was our standard weekend dinner, which ended much too quickly.

While Mom took a call from a client, Dad and I opened the crawl space and ducked inside. The box from the Council wasn't really a box; it was a chest. A very cool and extremely heavy chest. Dad insisted on helping me load it into the car before I headed home. I lingered, not wanting the moment of normalcy to end.

"Acacia will come with me next week. She misses you guys and she needs some fatherly guidance. Remind her that she can't just leach off her sister for the rest of her days."

He laughed and hugged me again. "I'm sorry, Arabella. You should have had this a long time ago. I thought I was doing the right thing by letting you live the life you wanted."

"You did, Dad. Thank you."

Chapter Six

Cassie and I treated Eve with a spa day while the others worked on her surprise birthday party. For once, she hadn't made a big deal about her special day. This was saying a lot since Eve lived to entertain and spoil everyone else. It was time to return her affections.

The last spa day and birthday party combo had turned into a disaster of epic proportions, which coincidentally brought us to the fact most of Eve's party guests were now undead. The more Rowan told me to stop calling the reborn 'undead', the more I desperately wanted to keep doing it. Regardless of the word used, this was why we were dragging our feet so the sunless quartet could get the decorations up before we got home.

We'd finished our massages and sauna treatments and were now getting primed and polished. Not a terrible way to spend the afternoon and evening. No mention of the Immortal Council or living immortals was a small blessing. The snacks from a local bakery were pretty good too. I'd stuffed myself on turkey croissant sandwiches and chocolate cannoli.

"Do you think I should go with crimson or blush, Cassie?" Eve leaned over with the nail polish samples.

"The pink one." Cassie pointed.

"What are you getting?" Eve asked.

"Buff and shine. These nails actually do work." Cassie shot a dazzling smile my way.

I had to force the frown but it didn't last. It had actually been a pretty nice girls' day. My sister was missing out and as much as she annoyed me, I knew Eve wished she was here with us too. These were the kinds of things I wanted to make sure Eve enjoyed before she was limited by the sun, as well as all the frickin' Council rules. So many rules!

"Oh, I work, Cas. Who do you think keeps those crazy people I live with in line? I mean, it would be blood baths every night without my oversight." The conversation in the room suddenly vanished and I remembered where I was. "Metaphorically, of course."

"Of course." Eve shared a look with Cassie then she changed the subject. "I'm thinking about changing my major."

"Aren't you almost done?" I asked.

Eve fidgeted in her chair. "Well, yeah but my long-term plans have changed. It's not like I'm really going to be able to use a degree in Literature anyway."

This time my frown was real. She knew she'd need an official position in the clan so she was changing her life so she'd fit. I didn't want anyone but my sweet Eve. We'd make it work. If nothing else, she could be Victor's handler. Someone needed to keep him in line and so far Rowan was doing a terrible job.

Cassie looked at me. "She kinda has a point. Maybe you can just add classes rather than starting over, like business or public relations?"

My phone buzzed and I carefully unlocked the screen as to not disturb my newly painted black and gold glitter nails. There was a text from Rowan.

We should be done within the hour.

I caught Cassie's eye and held up one finger letting her know we were approaching the final countdown. Eve was chatting with her manicurist about the best cuticle oil and missed our silent communication. I didn't even know cuticles needed oiling.

Cassie said her goodbyes at the spa. She actually did have to work in the morning so she wasn't coming to the second half of the party. Eve and I grabbed some gelato before we headed up the hill just to give the crew a few more minutes.

"Did you have a good birthday?" I asked then quickly licked my cone before it dripped onto my steering wheel.

41

"Of course! Summer semester has been killing me. A relaxation day was exactly what I needed. Thank you so much."

When we rounded the final bend in the drive, the strings of lights started to pop into view. They looked like tiny butterflies leading from the front door around to the side yard.

"What's that?" Eve asked.

"Why don't you go find out?" I couldn't help but smile.

She bounced from the car as I pulled it around the side to the garage. I parked outside next to Rowan's fully restored 1970's hearse and hurried to follow Eve to the party. His car had been abandoned in a barn when we'd been running from Seraphine's goons. He was ridiculously thrilled to have it back in his possession. Unfortunately, it attracted a lot of attention, so he didn't take it out much as he would have liked. We'd also purchased a black Suburban with light block windows for the clan to use when runs to town might end up longer than expected.

"Surprise!" Multiple voices yelled as Eve rounded the corner. "Happy birthday!"

Fairy lights were strung from the front of the house all the way to the side and surrounded the party space, creating a soft ring of light. The log picnic tables were adorned with pink and yellow flowers and dozens of flickering candles. The center table held a mountain of wrapped gifts and food. A gorgeous three-tiered chocolate cake was the centerpiece.

Eve beamed with joy and took turns hugging everyone. She spent so much time pleasing other people, it was a nice change to return the favor. Rowan approached me with a can of something.

"Nice work, Steward. Really earning your pay today," I teased him with a shoulder bump.

"Ara, I'd love to take credit but Dona is the mastermind behind this. She's been snooping on Eve's socials and spying on her mobile to make sure Eve didn't catch any FOMO."

Grinning at this attempt to use trendy lingo, I grabbed the can from his hand and took a swig then looked at the label. It was some sort of girly vodka drink but clearly, he had been adding more booze as he went. The can specified cherry as the flavor but all I tasted was vodka.

"Can I get one of these but without the five extra shots?"

Rowan bowed dramatically then backed away with a flourish. I shook my head and watched the party. Eve was opening presents with Acacia. Dona and Steve were arguing about how to set up the lawn darts. And then there was one, standing slightly apart from the rest.

Instead of letting him ruin my mood, I moved to inspect the cake. The thin layer of vanilla buttercream over the chocolate cake gave the appearance of quaking aspen bark with edible flowers cascading down the front like a waterfall. Why did I know so much about cakes? I'd spent hours looking at wedding cakes with Eve. That memory made my stomach hurt.

I reached out and took a swipe of the frosting off the back and wondered if I had to wait for Eve to have a piece. It was beyond delicious, not too sweet, not too tangy. My hand moved back for another taste.

"There's a practice cake inside if you don't want to wait." Victor's voice sounded from behind me.

I forced myself not to flinch then licked my fingers, seriously considering devouring the practice cake before turning to face him. "Don't lie. You bought this."

The corner of his mouth curved into a smile. "Actually, yes. I had planned on making something but I was overruled by Dona. She's very pushy for someone so small."

"Finally, something we can agree on."

Silence began to stretch and I wondered what was keeping Rowan. This should get easier eventually, right? Maybe the fact that the last thing I'd said to him was that I hated him didn't help.

"Can I talk to you for a second?"

"Isn't that what we're doing?"

I resisted the urge to roll my eyes. "I meant alone."

He nodded so I headed toward the back of the house. It was darker here but I could see better than ever in the low light. The first time I'd seen my eyes glow, it freaked me out big time. Away from the light pollution, stars exploded in the sky. One shot in an arc above us. This was the best perk of living way out here.

Once we were far enough from the party and the house, I laid down on the grass. Victor hesitated then sat next to me. The ground was a little damp but it felt nice against the warm air.

"I'm sorry about what I said the other night." I watched another star fall across the sky.

"If that's what you need, I can be that person for you."

I closed my eyes and rubbed them with the palms of my hands. "That's the thing, Victor. I don't *want* to need that person."

"Can I ask a question?"

"Isn't that what you just did?" I rolled onto my side and propped up on my elbow to face him.

"Why do you hate yourself?"

Yep. That was *the* question, wasn't it? I rolled back to face the sky once again because the answer sucked. A few minutes passed before I could put into words what I'd been feeling since I'd returned from California.

"Because I'm not *me* anymore. Everything I was, everything I worked for, is gone."

"We all start over at some point. Maybe this is your time."

I sat up and faced him. "It's really hard to hate you when you're honestly trying to talk sense into me. Can we just go back to fighting all the time?"

He chuckled and looked up at the stars. "Did you make a wish?"

I followed his gaze. Stars fell over and over across the cloudless sky. I didn't know what to wish for because I didn't know what I wanted.

Actually, I did, but that part of my life was over. Wishing on a falling star wasn't going to change that.

"Did you?" I asked to deflect.

"I already got my wish." He closed his eyes but kept his face turned toward the sky.

There really was something different about him. He seemed less intense, like the pressure of life wasn't weighing him down anymore. Probably because it was too busy crushing me but still. He was part of my clan and I'd need to figure out how to deal with him. Hating him wasn't healthy, so what else could I do?

I opened my mouth to ask what his wish was but stopped myself. The letter told me everything I needed and more. *If I live through this, I will spend the rest of my existence making up for all the wrongs I've done to you. My only wish is to be part of your life. However you choose, for as long as you choose.*

Okay, he was still a little intense. But maybe he was also a little right; now was my time to start over. The problem was I had no idea where to begin. Ever since that first night at Seraphine's, I had not made any of my own decisions and the ones I attempted to make were terrible. My life was tumbling out of control.

After a few moments, I tapped him gently on the arm. "Let's go see if it's cake time."

He opened his eyes and stared straight ahead. "I changed my mind. I wish for cake."

A laugh escaped my lips and once it started, I couldn't stop. Tears streamed down my cheeks as I tried to stop laughing. I wanted my entire life back and he would use his wish for a piece of cake. I didn't need someone to hate. I needed someone to put my fucked-up life into perspective.

• • • •

45

"I HAVE BEEN WAITING forever for this movie to come out!" Eve reminded me for the hundredth time tonight. "The book was really good so the movie can't be that bad, right?"

"Why are you buying so many snacks?" I asked. "Literally only two of us can eat them."

Eve ignored me and placed a second bag of gummy worms in the shopping cart, which already contained six bags of chips plus dip, two jumbo boxes of popcorn, and a half a dozen kinds of chocolate.

Steve followed us about ten paces back with his arms folded across this chest. I couldn't tell if he was going for menacing or nauseated. He really needed to get over his problem with crowds. There were only about a dozen people in the store, including the employees. I'd have left him home but I was tired of fighting with Rowan about it. Maybe the quick trip would help him realize not everyone was out to get us, or him.

"Listen, I know all you want is my French toast popcorn and chocolate cinnamon bears but I like variety," Eve said, adding a package of red licorice to our haul.

"Let's grab some more coffee and eggs while we're here." I suggested and took a left at the end of the aisle hoping to get her away from the junk food.

"I don't love freezer pizza but we didn't really have anything planned for dinner. Should I?" Eve took a step away but I grabbed her arm before she disappeared into the frozen food section.

"Eve, we're fine. I'm not really that hungry. Plus, there are still tons of leftovers from your birthday party."

"Fine." Her lip came out in a bit of a pout then she took off.

I shook my head and made my way toward the eggs. Steve followed silently behind. Eve reappeared a moment later with a box of frozen pretzels. I did my best not to roll my eyes as she dropped it into the cart.

"I know you don't love chick flicks but this one was advertised as a romantic thriller so it's the best of both worlds," Eve said as we got back to the car.

I was exhausted and planned on eating popcorn then crashing while the movie played. The Council meetings were draining and trying to get comfortable with Victor living in my house was a challenge to say the least.

The birthday party had been the easiest interaction we'd had since his return. Him walking into my room the following night as I was stepping out of the shower was not. Not sure if he got a full frontal or if my towel had covered at least part of me. He promised he'd knocked but I didn't believe him. Rowan kept telling me he was still trying to figure out the new boundaries. The problem was I didn't know where those were either.

Everyone at the house was joining us for Eve's big movie premier. She had been talking about this for months so, once again, she was making an event out of it. I was grateful for Steve's help to carry all the groceries in since Eve was on her phone when we got home.

Acacia was waiting for us in the kitchen. Eve grabbed the popcorn and got to work while I put away the cold things. I snagged a leftover piece of roast beef and popped it in my mouth. Apparently, I was hungrier than I thought so I ended up making myself a quick sandwich.

Eve and my sister worked together to get all the snacks prepped and moved to the screening room. I stayed out of the way and did a little dance while I enjoyed the meat and cheesy deliciousness. Once it was gone, I grabbed a ginger ale and made my way to the first lower level.

The screening room was set up with tiered recliners in sets of four, with a total of five rows. Eve had all the food on a folding table just to the side of the first row. She and Acacia were already seated and waiting. Rowan was messing with the surround sound while Dona nitpicked his adjustments. Steve sat in the back row nearest the door. So far Victor was a no show.

I grabbed a smaller bowl of popcorn and a box of chocolate covered almonds then sat on the opposite end of the second row from the girls. Adjusting my chair to the perfect position where I could still reach my drink, I tucked my snacks along the side. Dona turned down the lights and started the movie.

It was less than twenty minutes before my blinks started getting longer and longer. The werewolf love triangle was so overly dramatic that I was afraid I'd start giggling and hurt Eve's feelings. This really wasn't my kind of movie but it made Eve happy to have everyone together so I was here trying to sleep in a recliner rather than my own comfortable bed.

When I opened my eyes again, the room was quiet, which meant I slept through the rest of the movie and the sound of everyone leaving. Rather than getting up and crawling to my room, I snuggled in further with a sigh. These chairs were actually pretty comfy.

The sound of hushed footsteps pulled me back when I was ready to succumb to sleep once again. I really didn't want to talk to anyone so I kept my breathing slow and hoped whomever it was would leave me alone.

A light blanket was gently laid over me. My first thought was Dona since she took the Mother Hen role to another level. However, when I took a deep breath, I recognized Victor's cologne. My first impulse was annoyance but I continued to pretend to be asleep to see if he'd push too far.

Time ticked by and sleep once again started dragging me under. Dreams started shaping reality and I wasn't sure if I was still awake or not when Victor shifted my hair off my face.

"I don't know how to fix this." Victor's voice was barely a whisper. "You deserve the best in this fucked up world and as much as I hate to say it, that's not me."

It took everything I had to keep my breathing slow and steady. If he knew I was awake, I doubted he would keep going. He was silent again for so long that I almost opened my eyes.

"You have every right to hate me but I will spend the rest of my immortal life making sure you are safe and happy." A whisper of a kiss touched my forehead. "Sleep well, my Arabella."

His confession took a couple seconds to permeate my brain. "Victor, I don't..."

When I sat up and looked around, I was alone. However, the sound of the door being pulled closed told me I hadn't dreamed his words.

Chapter Seven

Acacia had been sullen since we left the very late dinner at our parents' house. I understood how she felt. It was easy when we were there, like old times. She put on a brave face but I knew she missed her old life too, not to mention Mom's meatloaf.

The feeling of nostalgia faded a bit more when we pulled up to the house. The contents of the chest would pull me further from my old life so I'd left it in the trunk. Probably not the best storage conditions but it had survived in the crawl space for years.

My sister had bailed as soon as I put the car in park. She clearly needed some space, which made me take my time following her inside. Lights were on all over and I heard voices from the kitchen. I also smelled something wonderful.

Once I got close, I could tell it was Eve and Victor talking and laughing. Quietly, I stopped at the entryway and watched. They were obviously baking something since the kitchen looked like it had exploded. Flour was everywhere, including all over them.

Eve was drizzling a glaze over something hidden by a mountain of ingredients while Victor watched. He had such pride in his expression and I remembered he taught her how to cook. When Eve lifted the glaze, it dribbled all over her hand and arm. They both started laughing and I couldn't help but smile. It was the most normal thing I'd ever seen Victor do. His adoration for his little sister was clear in this expression.

"Oh, Arabella! You're home!" Eve wiped her hands on her apron and came over to give me a hug.

I stepped back. "Eve, you're covered in flour and who knows what else. You're not going to ruin my only nice sundress."

She frowned then skipped back over to the counter and carefully picked up the something delicious they had made. "Blueberry scones with lemon poppy seed glaze. I've been working on this recipe for years and I think I finally nailed it."

I took a bite and closed my eyes with a moan. The crust was crisp but the still warm filling was perfectly baked. The sweet and tart were exquisitely balanced. I was rethinking my idea of making Victor house chef and giving that job to Eve instead.

"Do you need a moment alone with your scone, sis?"

Acacia had been sitting just out of sight and I jumped when she spoke. Clearly, she had recovered quickly from her moodiness. When I opened my eyes, Victor was washing dishes with purpose. Maybe I had enjoyed that a little too much in public and I felt a blush rise to my cheeks.

"Mind your business," I said around another bite. "You're just jealous."

She gave me a put-out look telling me I was right. "I'm going to go start the movie."

"Let me pop some popcorn and I'll be right there. Grab Dona and Steve on your way. They were both pretty excited to watch a movie about alien robots."

"Remember to tell her it is not real or she'll be terrified," I called as Acacia disappeared around the corner.

I plopped down at the breakfast bar and helped myself to another scone. Eve popped two bags of popcorn, sprinkled them with her secret spice blend that made it taste like nachos then disappeared. Victor was still cleaning up and putting stuff away.

"How are your parents?" he asked with his back turned.

"Fine. They're still weirded out by all the changes but it's nice to get away and forget about everything for a few hours."

The house was quiet and I should have joined the rest of them to watch the movie but I didn't. The surround sound in the screening room was awesome. The way it was blocked from the rest of the house meant I could watch my action flicks anytime I wanted without disturbing anyone. I needed to talk to Victor and this may be my only chance for some privacy before we left to meet with the Council.

I took my time eating a third scone while he meticulously cleaned the kitchen. Maybe he could be the housekeeper? The thought of him wearing a maid outfit made me giggle and almost choke on my treat. When he finally tossed the dish rag into the sink, I stood and the seriousness of our pending conversation wiped the grin from my face.

"We need to talk."

"Did you make a decision about the power of attorney?" he asked.

"No, it's not about that." I kept looking at the line of flour just above his right eyebrow and I couldn't concentrate so I walked over and gently wiped it off.

"I think you should go watch the movie." Victor had closed his eyes and stepped back.

"Don't give me an out. If you haven't noticed, this is hard on me too." I tried to make it sound lighthearted but it fell flat. "I really do need to talk to you about something."

He opened his eyes and looked down at his flour covered shirt. "Fine, but I need to change."

I followed him as he made his way down to the third basement level. Only a few rooms were finished this far down. They were supposed to be for visiting living immortals and councilmembers. The shit Seraphine fed everyone for years about immortal clans being enemies was bull. We were supposed to be working together and when one was in the area, it was expected that the living immortal would host them for an undisclosed amount of time. Which, in short meant, I could have house guests with no notice for as long as they wished to stay. Man, I missed living alone.

Victor had moved into one of the two-room suites, pretty much the farthest distance from my rooms as possible. He had set up the living space as mostly an office but had a flat screen up on the wall across from a very comfy looking recliner big enough for two. I peeked in the other room but did not enter. The bedroom was nearly as large as mine. There was a chance this room was specifically designed for

Immortal Council but whatever, no one told me if certain rooms were off limits.

This was not a conversation for a bedroom. However, it was a private conversation so I pulled the door to the hallway closed then jumped when I heard music. The crisp clarity that could only be vinyl drew me into the other room. Victor had changed into clean pants and was buttoning up his shirt when I entered. He stopped midway up and I forced myself to look away. This was not going to be easy.

Here goes nothing.

"I've completed the final binding with everyone in my clan, except you. The Council gave me an extension due to your absence but I would feel better if it were done before we met with them again."

"Okay. What does it entail?" he asked as he rolled up his sleeves.

He knew. The look on his face told me he knew exactly what needed to happen and the bastard was going to make me spell it out. "The living immortal must take the reborn's blood and the reborn must take theirs. It's like a contract, business really."

"And you've done this with the rest of the clan?" His voice was not even but I couldn't tell what emotion was trying to break through.

"Yes. It was awkward but after I felt closer to everyone. They're my family now."

"And you aren't sure if you want me to be your family?" A hint of what sounded like anger slipped through and I suddenly wondered if Rowan should be here.

I rolled my shoulders back and took a step forward. "I made the decision to keep you in my clan. That hasn't changed."

"But?" he asked when I didn't immediately continue.

I clenched my fists and pressed on. "Before when I had to take your blood, you seemed... uncomfortable. The truth is, so was I."

This confession seemed to genuinely surprise him. "Because of how much you hate me?"

I sat on the chair next to the record player and watched the needle bob up and down. I'd been blaming Victor for everything bad that had happened over the last two years. If I were completely honest with myself, I made the decisions, the good and the bad. He may have forced my hand on occasion but ultimately, I was to blame for where I was today. Mostly, anyway.

"If I don't make you an official part of my clan, you'll be considered a rogue and you're already in enough hot water with the Council. I had a hunch that was what Pierre intended all along. He wanted me to reject you on the spot so he had a reason to kill you. Permanently. Once I started learning about the immortal clans, my suspicions were confirmed. I don't want to hate you, Victor, but we can't go back or forget our past."

The music changed to something far too familiar. It felt like a lifetime ago when he told me his favorite song, yet here it was. I wondered if he thought about it when he started the music just now.

"You're right, but we can choose how to move forward. I've never had to work for the things I've wanted so I don't really know how, especially when it comes to people. My persuasion gave me a false reality of my own design. None of my previous relationships had any substance, with the exception of Rachel and we both know how that turned out. The mistakes I made with you aren't forgivable but I'm going to try to win your forgiveness nevertheless." Victor held out his hand. "Dance with me?"

"That would require you to touch me." I forced a laugh then met his eyes.

There was no persuasion in his voice. He was leaving this decision entirely up to me. He had asked me months ago to trust him, maybe it was time to try. I took his hand and let him take me into his arms. It felt very wrong, and very right. This was my fear. Something had happened while we were on the run. I couldn't explain it but it happened.

I rested my head against his shoulder and let him guide the dance. We spun slowly and I tried to reconcile my decisions and his statement about forgiveness. He'd been nothing but honest with me and I needed to follow suit if we were going to make whatever this was work.

"How did it make you feel?" His words were quiet yet somehow pleading and my feet stilled at the emotion.

"Like I was tired of being angry," I whispered, still not making eye contact, "like I could be wanted and loved for who I am now."

His grip tightened because I'd either said the wrong or the right thing. He let me go and stepped back. "The binding is a contract, nothing more."

I swallowed and nodded. "Let's get it over with then?"

We sat on the edge of the bed. I suddenly felt like an awkward teenager about to get her first kiss. I took a deep breath to steel my resolve. *This is a business contact. This is just a business contract.*

When I'd shared blood with the other clan members, we had cut ourselves and drank from wine glasses. This had been Rowan's suggestion. There was an intimacy that came with sharing blood directly that was not part of the contractual agreement. It had still been awkward but after it was done, we had all laughed. I felt closer to everyone and the tension in the house dropped significantly. It was as if they expected me to turn away from them at any moment. The truth was more likely I would turn my back on myself, but that option no longer existed.

Victor didn't need to know any of this, or maybe Rowan has already told him. I took his hand in mine and bit down on his wrist. Emotions exploded around me as I pulled on the sweet elixir. That was another reason for the glasses. Living immortals craved reborn blood. It was like a drug and I always wanted just a bit more. My mind wandered back to the first time and all the emotions, to what I had almost done. Victor said something and I had to force myself to stop so I could listen.

"Your scars are gone," he said.

I lifted my hand to my neck and pushed my hair back. He meant the scars he had given me the first time he took my blood. It felt like a million years ago. His reborn blood made most of my other scars disappear but not those. After the binding ceremonies, I noticed they had all but faded. You couldn't erase the scars you created.

"Let's finish this." My voice was thick and I needed to leave before I made more bad decisions.

Victor shifted his body and put his arm around me. I held my breath as his lips brushed my neck in what felt very much like a kiss. Still, I felt none of his persuasion leading me down a path I couldn't come back from. At this point, I was afraid I didn't need the push. Heat flashed across my skin, followed by goosebumps in the anticipation of what I knew was coming next.

The shuddering sigh that escaped my lips spoke volumes. This was not a good idea. As he pulled, I let myself drown in the desire that rolled off him in waves. I leaned my body into his and reveled in his touch. When he moved to pull away, I held on for one more second, not wanting to lose the personal connection. For the first time since I could remember, I didn't feel alone.

My tangled emotions warred with my rational brain. The binding was over but my way forward was still a blur. If I kept on my current path, I would continue to drown in sadness over what I'd lost with Tom and the normal life that could never be. I'd be trapped in a loop of anger and despair for eternity. There would be no sharing coffee while watching the sunrise or children to raise. Tears pricked my eyes for everything I hadn't realized I wanted until it was gone.

But I had another choice. A choice standing right in front of me. Could I forgive the past so I could have a chance for happiness in this life that was thrust upon me? That road wouldn't be an easy one. Maybe I wouldn't be able to let go of the hurt he'd caused me. Maybe it would end just like with Tom once Victor realized what I'd become or when he had the realization of being trapped with me for a lifetime when a lifetime for us could be centuries.

"You should go." His voice was raspy and he almost trembled against my touch.

"Victor, I don't..." I squeezed my eyes closed and tried to find reason but there was only emotion. "I don't think I want to."

He bolted to his feet and paced to the other side of the room. "I can't give you what you want."

"Why? Suddenly now, when I'm the one asking, it's not okay?" I moved to stand in front of him and tried to make eye contact, but he avoided me. His hand fisted in the material of my dress as he clenched his jaw as if he couldn't help but touch me now that I'd allowed it. "What aren't you telling me? Victor, what was your punishment from the Council? Rowan won't tell me."

"I can't either." He finally met my gaze, and I saw a man at war with himself.

I folded my arms across my chest. "As clan leader, I have a right to know."

He hesitated but I wasn't going to give in. "I took from them what they wanted most, a new living immortal. It has been a very long time since one was born and they were getting two until I came along. So, they took from me the one thing I wanted more than anything else. You."

Blood rushed in my ears and words fell from my lips, against my better judgement. "And if I disagree?"

"Arabella, this isn't you talking. It's the blood sharing. You were never in control in life, and you definitely aren't now."

He moved to change the record, his movements stiff as if he was in pain. I sat on the edge of the bed and considered his words. What he said, while true, felt like an excuse. As if he was convincing himself as much as me.

My reaction to blood sharing was not something I could control. I'd never had to separate blood lust from regular lust so what was the point of learning to fight it? But at this moment, I didn't care. I was flat out tired of all the rules. Either I was going to start living my life or I was going to continue to spiral into the darkness. This moment would change everything but I knew this leap was what I needed to start moving forward instead of staying stuck in the past.

I stood then laid my hand on his back, making him freeze. "And if I demand it?"

Suddenly my back was against the wall, his body pressed against mine. "You swore you would never do that to me again."

I licked my lips and leaned in. "Then don't make me."

Chapter Eight

The faint lamp light was in the wrong place when I woke up. The bed felt too soft and what was with all these pillows? Fingers traced tiny circles on my back. The memories came in a rush and instead of tensing, my body relaxed into the comfort. I'd spent the entire night making love to the man I was supposed to hate.

Once it was clear I wasn't leaving, he'd given in without too much of a fight. Honestly, I'd imagined a quickie to dispel the tension between us. Victor had other plans. He's spent hours making good on all those promises in his letter. In that time, I let my body trick my mind into believing maybe I was worth loving again.

He kissed the center of my back, sending tingles down to my toes. "I always knew you'd be the death of me."

I rolled over and studied him. It should be a sin to look that sexy when someone first woke up. His dark hair was tousled, where I'm sure mine looked like a rat's nest. In the low light, his blue eyes almost glowed. He leaned in tentatively and I met him halfway. His tender kiss held unspoken words but I didn't want to think right now. I just needed to feel alive.

Instead, I shifted my body so I could wrap my leg over his hip. My arms tightened around his neck as my lips trailed along his stubbled jaw line down to his throat, skimming my fangs along the corded muscle there. Sound rumbled in his chest and I shivered as heat curled low in my belly.

When I loosened my grip to slide my hands lower, he flattened me on my back and held my hands above my head. My head spun as I forgot to breathe while his mouth ravaged mine. His hard length was pinned between us and I tilted my hips, begging for more. Another growl from deep in his chest and he plunged inside me. In this moment, the real world didn't matter and I let myself drown in make-believe.

Hours later, I realized there was no way to keep this secret. At minimum Rowan and Dona had come looking for me since they had real issues of giving me any alone time. Rowan would find my car and know I was still on the grounds. He wouldn't have to think too hard to know where to look next.

My sundress did not survive the encounter so I snagged one of Victor's navy-colored dress shirts. It was whisper soft and just long enough to cover my important bits. After rolling up the sleeves, I peeked out the door. There was a tray with a tall glass of orange juice, sliced strawberries, three of Eve's delicious scones, and a piece of paper folded in half. I picked it up and read the note.

Arabella, I've taken everyone out for karaoke. Enjoy your night. You both deserve it. Remember you promised not never, just not yet. ~Eve

"Your sister is a devious little shit, isn't she?" I asked as I brought the tray into the living area, pausing long enough to appreciate Victor's bare chest and low-slung black pajama pants.

"Very." After reading the note, he sighed. "What did you promise her?"

The scone suddenly turned to ash in my mouth and I knew I'd made a mistake giving it to him. "Um, she wants to begin the transition for rebirth?"

I hated that it came out as a question. I hated it even more when his expression meant my evening alone might end up being just that. My butt hit the floor next to where I'd set the tray. I didn't want to risk getting crumbs in the fancy recliner.

"And you didn't tell her no?"

I swallowed my bite and stood, plucking the note from his hand and tapping him on the chest with it. "Here's the thing, Vic. It's not really your decision to make. I don't want to grow my clan but I don't want to lose Eve either. She's my best friend and clearly has both our interests at heart."

He shook his head then leaned in to kiss the tip of my nose. "My God, you're gorgeous when you're mad."

I rolled my eyes and sat back on the floor with a huff. "I take everything back. I still hate you."

Without warning, I was pinned to the ground. Victor's eyes held none of the earlier annoyance, instead mischief sparkled in their blue depths. "You keep saying hate but I think you mean the other four letter word."

Love? my panicked brain filled in.

Maybe lust or even slightly like but love was so far out of the picture, I couldn't even comprehend it. Luckily, he'd decided to convince me of this other four-letter word by kissing me breathless again.

When he finally let up, I spoke quickly. "There's a loophole, you know."

He picked up a scone and almost took a bite before frowning. "A loophole for scones?"

I plucked the pastry from his hand then licked the glaze off his finger. "No, for your punishment. As clan leader, I can assign you as Consort."

"Consort? Like your lover on paper?"

"Sounds gross when you say it like that..."

"It won't work." He roughly pushed his fingers through his hair. "Arabella, there isn't a way around this, and any minute I'm going to wake up to find this has been just another cruel dream."

I pinched his toe as hard as I could. "Sorry, pal. Not dreaming. We go back to the Immortal Council tomorrow. Looks like you have twenty-four hours to find a nonexistent loophole because I'm not coming back without you. You are seriously the only person as messed up as I am. I need you around to keep my sanity."

• • • •

AS I PASSED THE KITCHEN, I heard the TV. The intro music told me it was for one of those paparazzi shows that masqueraded as actual news. I wanted a glass of water so I tiptoed in thinking someone had left it on by mistake.

Acacia was sitting at the table with a glass of orange juice watching the screen. I looked down at my attire and cursed myself for not changing before wandering all over the house. Maybe I could get my water and leave before she turned? The TV was unusually loud.

"Here's an update on everyone's favorite mystery couple," the female broadcaster announced. "We all thought he was headed to the altar earlier this year but now we see there's another woman. And boy, are they getting cozy!"

My eyes slipped to the screen to see stills of Tom and Rachel. There were pictures at a café, a park, and snuggled together in a cab. When the boy was pictured with them, they looked like a perfect, happy family. The glass slipped from my fingers and shattered on the floor.

Acacia shot out of the chair and pressed the remote to turn off the TV. "Shit! I thought you were asleep."

"And I thought you were out with Eve. Can you get the broom? I don't have shoes on."

Acacia grabbed the broom and dustpan from the cupboard and brought it my way. She stopped just out of reach and took a moment to take in my wardrobe, or lack thereof. After a second of hesitation, she swept around me so I had a path around the center island.

"That's not really how we were going to let you know," she said as she piled the glass into the dustpan. "I'm sorry."

I got another cup out of the cabinet and filled it with water. The first slipped from my hand in shock but now I didn't know how to feel. I made the choice to walk away and was the one who pushed them back together. What did I think was going to happen? Plus, there was the whole Victor thing now; whatever *that* was. When had my life gotten so complicated?

"How long have you known?" I asked as I sat at the kitchen table.

"A couple of months. To start with, the stories just looked like Tom was building something with his kid but now... Well, you saw."

I took a long drink. "Yeah."

"You okay?" She sat next to me.

"Acacia, I don't really know how to feel about anything anymore. I keep making terrible decisions then acting like they're someone else's fault."

"Like sneaking around the house in Victor's shirt?"

I pushed her over. "Yeah, like that. Can we keep this between us for a bit? I'm not really sure how I feel about that yet either."

"What are sisters for?" She pushed me back. "But seriously, be careful. That dude is scary in love with you."

"Tell me about it." I changed the subject before I could dwell on her words too much. "I'm leaving tomorrow night to meet with the Council. Dad gave me this weird chest from them, do you want to go through it with me?"

"Sure, but can I tell you something first?" She wrinkled her nose at me. "You reek like Victor's cologne."

Chapter Nine

Acacia helped me drag the chest upstairs where I quickly showered and changed into a pair of shorts and a baggy t-shirt. I stuffed Victor's shirt in the bottom of my dresser so Dona wouldn't find it when she stole my laundry. I've told her a dozen times I was more than capable of washing my own clothes. Her solution was to randomly sneak in and do it when I wasn't paying attention. Actually, if she didn't get on it soon, I'd have no clean underwear for my trip.

I knelt in front of the chest and pressed the latches to unlock it. Dust poofed out as the seal released. We looked at each other. With my luck and current trend of bad choices, there was a chance we were opening Pandora's box.

I gently lifted the lid and peeked inside. No demons or malevolent beings spewed forth, just a bunch of papers and photographs. There was an envelope with my name written in a very fancy script on top. When I flipped it over, it was sealed with an ornate 'C' pressed into the red wax. I opened it carefully and held it out so we could both read it.

Dearest Arabella,

It is time you began learning of your place in this world. By now you must know there is something different, something remarkedly special about you. We have waited so very long for your birth. You are one of the most unique creatures on Earth. You, my dear, are a living immortal. A gift more precious than you yet realize.

This chest has your lineage chart as well as information to start your training. We at the Immortal Council wish you a full and productive life but when that mortal life ends, we will be ready to accept you into the fold.

Councilman Chatelain

"Wow. They're kinda full of themselves, aren't they?" Acacia asked as I passed over the letter.

"You have no idea," I mumbled.

I pulled out a leather-bound book and started flipping through the pages. There was a family tree that went back generations. Two names caught my eye: Seraphine and Pierre Chatelain.

"Great, we're related to crazy people." I made a gagging sound and set the book aside as my bedroom door opened.

"Knock, knock," Eve said as she poked her head in.

"Come on in. We're looking at the spooky chest my dad gave me from the Immortal Council."

She knelt beside us and poked at the contents of the box. After flipping through a stack of photos, she looked at me. "Can I talk to you for a second?"

"I already know." Acacia was unrolling scrolls and using my candles as paper weights.

"Know what?" Eve's voice was higher than normal.

"That my sister is whoring it up with her arch enemy."

Eve looked like she might faint and I wanted to slap my sister. "Wow, Acacia! Why don't you tell me how you really feel about it?"

She shrugged and unrolled another scroll. "I told you from the start, he has a creeper vibe."

I turned back to Eve. "Thanks for running interference. I'd rather talk to Rowan about it privately. It's a bit complicated."

"Talk to me about what, Love?" Rowan asked as he walked in.

"Aren't these supposed to be my private rooms?"

There was a light rap on my door and Dona poked her head in. "I'm just here to grab laundry and pack for your trip."

I threw my hands up in the air. "You know what? Everybody out. Rowan, you stay. Everyone else out!"

"But—" Acacia whined while pointing at the scrolls.

"Beat it."

Dona ran in, snagged my laundry bin, then disappeared behind the girls. For once, I was grateful for her help but I was packing for my own trip. Thank you very much!

Rowan made himself comfortable in one of the oversized chairs in the seating area. The chairs were big enough I could curl up and take a nap in them. He had slid down, crossed his ankles, and closed his eyes while I started putting things back in the chest. It would have to wait.

When I snapped the latch shut, he spoke. "You want me to start looking for a work around for our pal Victor's sentence?"

I had been squatting but fell back on my butt at his words. "You know too?"

"My dear Ara, it was inevitable. I wasn't one hundred percent sure when Eve suddenly offered to take us all out for a night of singing but once I found what was left of your yellow dress in Victor's rooms, my suspicions were confirmed."

I put my face in my hands. "That went around fast. Do Dona and Steve know?"

Rowan shook his head. "It's not their job to watch you two like it is mine. They will catch on eventually. You know I adore you, but you can't lie or keep a secret to save your life."

"Thanks," I huffed.

He sat up and finally made eye contact with me. "All that being said, you both are about to be put under the proverbial microscope. The Council was nearly evenly split on what to do with Victor and the other option was a slow and painful final death. It would not take much for them to reconsider."

"I'm still confused about how they get to control my personal life. Who I have sex with is none of their damn business."

"Arabella, your actions just condemned Victor to death. That idiot went willingly because of how irrational he is about you."

A chill fell over me as the words sunk in. "Why didn't he tell me?"

"Because that was part of the sentence. I'm not supposed to tell you either but the Council has really overstepped this time. The good news is the binding is complete for your entire clan. It's something they will be asking about in the update." Rowan gestured to the chest. "You should spend some time getting caught up on that. I'll keep everyone otherwise occupied until the sun comes up. I think you'll be surprised at what all the Council assumes they can control."

After he left, I started pulling the books, scrolls, and photos out of the chest and organizing them. Some of the scrolls looked really old, faded, and hard to read while others looked brand new. I'd covered a lot of this history with Dona but it appears there were things that were only shared with other living immortals, not their clan members. I'd been flying by the seat of my pants; it was time to do some serious research.

I flipped through the lineage book and made note of the different branches. It appeared all the living immortals stemmed from seven original vampires. This is why the Council is still made up of seven members, even though the family trees did come together a time or two. Incest was part of most royal families so why would vampires be any different? The good news was my tree seemed to have little of that.

Around noon, I found a book that was very interesting, so I curled up in my comfy chair to read more. It described the differences between living immortals and the reborn, as well as different genders of each. One overwhelming theme was living immortals did not partner up with reborn, unless it was part of a temporary Consort assignment.

The book slipped from my lap sometime later, landing on the floor with a dull thump. Clearly, I had fallen asleep. After a good stretch, I headed to the bathroom. My sleep schedule was non-existent anymore and I really had no idea what day or time it was without Dona.

The display on my digital clock read nine-thirty PM. Dona had snuck back in during my nap and all my clothes were either hung or neatly folded in my closet. I checked the bottom drawer. Victor's shirt was still there but now was neatly folded. So much for her not finding it.

My suitcase was open and already mostly full. I poked through what she had packed, leaving most of it in there. I grabbed a different pair of pajamas, stuffed in a pair of flip flops, and wished I had another sundress. Maybe Eve had something I could borrow.

Our flight was still several hours away so I changed into some workout clothes and hit the treadmill. An hour later, I was fully awake and ready for more reading, after a shower of course.

Once clean, I checked my phone. There was another voicemail from Tom. Eventually, we were going to have to talk. Next to my phone was a tray with what smelled like a caramel mocha, a turkey and avocado sandwich, and a folded note. I picked up the sandwich and read the note as I took a bite.

I would have brought ice cream but I was afraid it would melt, just like my heart. ~V

I looked back at my phone and swallowed hard. What had I gotten myself into? I'd thought about what happened with Victor during my run. My brain was trying to convince me that it was just the blood lust that made me do it, but I was lying to myself.

I did it because I was lonely and hurting, and for one minute I wanted to be accepted and adored for who I was. That was unfair to him but it was the truth. I walked away from the man I had loved so that he could have the life he couldn't have with me. My life was out of my control but last night I made a decision for myself, consequences be damned. Now that I had a clearer head and more information, I was second guessing myself. My moment of selfishness could take Victor's life. That thought brought an ache to my chest that I wasn't ready to digest.

After moving the tray next to my comfy chair, I grabbed a book from the bottom of the chest and started to read. Ignoring my problems always made them go away, right?

This book was creepy. It had history Dona never touched on and I wondered if this is what Rowan had wanted me to know before I met with the Council. The Immortal Council had their hands in everything from religion, being business partners with the biggest industries, and they even dabbled in politics at the highest level. This gave them access to people and places without question. At the end of the book was a list of names and contact information for more major cities and countries than I even recognized.

One of the names stuck out as it did not have a surname attached. The line just read: Joseph, Stewart for Councilman Chatelain, and a phone number. I added it to my contacts list and put the book away.

My thinking that this was a cult was not too far off. There were more living immortals than I realized based on these twenty plus year old books but in the grand scheme, there were only a few of us in a sea of billions. No wonder the Council had punished Victor for killing one.

Chapter Ten

Rowan insisted Steve drove us to the airport. Once we were out of sight of the house, he and I switched places. Steve wasn't a bad driver but he was just so dang slow and made a point to stop at yellow lights. We were on a tight schedule and my nerves could not deal with his sloth speed tonight. A private jet was waiting for us when we arrived. I gave Steve a quick goodbye hug then went to the cargo hatch to grab my bag. By the time I got there, Victor had both his and mine in his hands.

We hadn't had a chance to talk since I left his suite early this morning and now it felt awkward. Like roommates that had gotten drunk and fooled around but now were stuck together with a long lease agreement. Yeah, that was pretty much it except I was the house and breaking the lease meant death. No pressure, right?

I sat next to the window while Victor poured us both a glass of champagne and joined me. I took the glass then looked back outside, staring at nothing beyond my reflection in the glass. There was something else I had been putting off and I needed to stop procrastinating and rip off the proverbial band aid.

Victor spoke to break the silence as it continued to stretch. "The last time I was in Salt Lake City, there wasn't much time for sightseeing. I do know a great restaurant, as long as you get the right server."

"The baby wasn't yours." My voice was lower than I intended and I was still facing the window.

He didn't respond so I turned in case he hadn't heard me. Victor swirled the glass as he stared at the bubbles within. His hard expression told me everything. He deserved to know but I wasn't sure the information helped either of us move forward.

"You shouldn't have been punished for something you didn't know about. I didn't even know I was pregnant until I was in recovery. I still can't figure out how the Council found out."

He tipped up and drained his glass. "I know, but the how doesn't matter anymore. What's done is done."

"It matters to me."

Victor leaned toward me and held my gaze. "Don't pull on that thread, Arabella. It'll take you places you don't want to go. The sentence has been passed and I'll live with the consequences of my actions."

"Consequences made worse by my uninformed decisions. If I had known..." I started but he shook his head ever so slightly and pointed upward.

The jet was bugged. We were being listened to and probably watched. I glanced around the cabin and didn't see anything obvious but my dealings with the Council were significantly less than Victor's. I'd have to trust him on this one.

I took a sip of the champagne and grimaced. It was awful. "Any chance there's some ginger ale over there?"

No ginger ale. Luckily, the flight was just over an hour and a half so I used the time to check my email while Victor, not so subtly, watched me. I let out a deep breath when I was finally outside. The air smelled funny and I sneezed.

"You get used to it." Victor laughed and motioned for me to follow him to the airport long-term parking area.

"Wait. This can't be the one I saw in your garage, is it?" I asked when he stopped in front of a fully restored black and silver Mustang.

"The very same. I had a lot of time on my hands during my transition. Compared to some of my other hobbies, finishing the restoration on the Mustang seemed a good use of that time. Somehow, Seraphine's goons never made it to my house."

"But why is it here?" I asked once we were both in the car.

"I made a friend and he was able to make some requests on my behalf. There were only a few things from my old life that I cared about and now that the car is here, they are all back with me."

I wondered if he included me on that list but maybe I was over-thinking his statement. When I met his gaze, I changed my mind. It was clear that I was on that short list but I wasn't sure how I felt about that yet. He turned over the engine and the beast roared, in a good way. I wanted to get behind the wheel of this baby but I could wait.

"Once you drive this, you will never look at your fiberglass wanna-be Mustang the same way."

"Hang on there, Vic. Don't go bashing my car. I could beat this bucket of bolts any day."

He smiled and backed out. "I can't wait for you to try."

The drive from the airport to the city proper only took a few minutes. We toured downtown for a bit with him pointing out places of interest. Considering he hadn't had any time to sightsee, he knew a lot about the city. When we drove by the temple, I was very impressed. I'd only seen pictures and they did not give the building the justice it deserved.

"Don't worry, you'll get a closer look tomorrow."

I laughed but he glanced my way. "You're not serious?"

"Are you hungry or did you want to go straight to the hotel?" he asked.

"Is the hotel bugged?"

"Most definitely." He gripped the steering wheel harder.

"I could eat."

I watched people slowly making their way through downtown. Victor got turned around during the trip to the restaurant with all the one-way streets but I wasn't in any hurry. We passed a small concert venue and I did a double take. Tom was playing here tomorrow night. I never listened to the newest voicemail, now I wish I had.

We parked about half a block from the restaurant. Victor opened my door and offered his hand, which I took without a second thought. Once I was on the sidewalk beside him, he gave it a slight squeeze before letting go. I smiled despite myself at the sweet gesture. We'd only made it a few feet when I heard my name.

"Arabella?"

I looked across the street and froze. Tom was holding his son's hand and Rachel was a step behind him. We made eye contact for a second then she looked to my left. All the color drained from her face and she took a step so she was half-behind Tom. I'd forgotten about her and Victor's past until that moment.

I waved and Tom jogged across the busy street, leaving the two of them standing alone. Victor kept walking toward the restaurant. Tom wrapped me in a hug that I carefully returned but quickly pulled out of.

He glanced in the direction Victor had gone then asked, "It's so great to see you. Why are you in Utah?"

"Business. Complicated business." I started, then changed the subject. "But how are you? I'm sorry I didn't get a chance to call you back."

"I've been crazy busy with the tour and Tommy. I guess you met him at the hospital."

"Sort of, yeah."

The streetlight popped above us and suddenly we were shrouded in darkness. When I caught his eye again, his expression faltered, and his posture stiffened. What I saw there was fear. My eyes must be glowing. I blinked and his expression was back to normal, making me wonder if it had been my imagination. In my heart though, I knew that was a lie. His feelings about my kind were very clear.

He was never going to accept what I'd become. Our chance was over, even if we hadn't said the words out loud. It should have hurt more but if I was honest with myself, it was over the moment I walked out of his hospital room. I wasn't worth what he'd have to give up to be with me and I was strong enough to accept that. Didn't mean I had to be happy about it though.

I looked back across the street to see Rachel and Tommy watching us. "It was nice to see you, Tom, but you'd better get back."

He pulled me in for another hug, gave me a peck on the cheek, then whispered, "I miss you."

I closed my eyes and stepped back, not allowing myself to read too much into his words. "I'll call soon."

With that, I quickly walked away. Seeing a still shot on TV was different than running into them in real life. I'd felt nothing that night, but I felt something now: overwhelming jealousy. She had everything I used to want and if I was going to move forward with my life, I'd have to let that dream go.

I wiped away an angry tear and yanked the restaurant door open. The hostess smiled at me but I spotted Victor before she finished her welcome speech. I hurried to the table and sat across from him, trying not to wrap my arms around my body to keep from falling apart. Clinging to my past was not going to help me accept my future.

Victor was holding the drink list and I tried to focus on the food menu but words were suddenly too hard. The smell of food made my stomach roll. How dare Tom try to pull me back in? I walked away so he could have the chance for the normal life I'll never have. How could I feel all these emotions at once?

"Hi. My name is Marty. I'll be your server tonight. Oh hello, handsome. It's so nice to see you again."

This made me look up in time to see Victor rearrange his features from murderous to stony. His discomfort gave me something else to focus on. I needed this backstory and a stiff drink. Anything to distract me from the current crushing self-doubt.

I spoke to the server while Victor tried to strangle the drink menu. "Hi Marty. I'm new. What's good here?"

He turned to me. "Oh, aren't you the cutest! He always brings Mr. Serious. I'm glad he's found some new friends. The crab dip is to die for and we have a new spicy chicken pasta. So yummy."

"We'll have both and a double apple martini."

Marty frowned as Victor spoke. "She's from out of town. She'll have a regular apple martini and when it's gone, bring out my usual."

Marty made a note on his pad then winked at Victor before sauntering away. I bit my bottom lip to keep from laughing. What I wouldn't give for a few moments alone with Marty to get some dirt on Victor, and who was Mr. Serious?

"This must be what you meant about this place being nice depending on the server. Marty seems super fun."

Victor pinched the bridge of his nose. "Except I meant it was nice when he's not here. He's a bit much but honestly, always provides great service. You can't order a double anything and I'm glad you said 'we' rather than 'I' or I would have had to order food for myself. Please don't encourage him."

"There you go trying to make decisions for me again. I think Marty and I are going to be besties."

Victor looked me dead in the eye. "How was your talk with Tom?"

I flicked the paper ring from my silverware at him. "Not cool, Vic. Not cool. But, hey, thanks for leaving me standing alone on the sidewalk. Dona and Rowan will love that."

"I have nothing else to say to him."

Huh? This was news to me. The last time the three of us had been in a room together, they had been trying to mend their strained relationship. What would drive a wedge between them again? My first thought was that Victor wanted Rachel back, but then it hit me. There were only a few people who knew I was pregnant: me, the hospital staff, and Tom. Tom had told the Immortal Council about the baby.

"Here's your apple-tini and shh, here's your wine." He winked at Victor again then placed two glasses and a bottle of red wine on the table. Before he left, he spoke in a singsong voice and said, "Drink your cocktail quick so I don't get in trouble."

Once he was out of earshot, I turned back to Victor. "Okay, what the fuck?"

Victor's lips twitched in a smile. "Utah has some backward liquor laws. I'll explain later but you really should drink that martini quickly."

I put the glass to my lips and sipped the sour apple goodness. It did go down very quickly but I didn't get my usual buzz. Something told me that the vodka was a little sparse.

Victor leaned forward. "We need to go over a few things before we meet with the Council tomorrow."

"Yeah, later at the hotel so we can have a private conversation now."

"Okay, what did you want to talk about?" he asked, folding his hands on the table.

I motioned between the two of us. "Did I really put your life at risk? Eve, Acacia, Rowan, *and* Dona already know. It's not going to take long to get back to the Council."

He took my hands and looked at me. "It was worth it."

I blushed and pulled my hands back. "Not helpful. Did you find a loophole or not?"

"Arabella, I already told you, there are none. They made sure of that when they sentenced me. I used the only trump card to save my life. I doubt another will just appear out of thin air."

I rocked back in my chair. "Well, fuck."

"Couldn't have said it better myself." He lifted his glass and I grabbed mine then touched them in cheers.

The food was delicious and I was able to convince Marty to bring me one more apple-tini before we left. My earlier melancholy was starting to ease. I had hoped to get a few minutes alone with Marty for some backstory but Victor made sure he couldn't share too much.

When we exited the restaurant, a grimy looking small dog streaked across the road. A car squealed to a stop and the driver yelled out the window. The pup ran straight toward Victor. To my surprise, he leaned over and gave the mutt a scratch between the ears as the little guy wiggled from head to toe with absolute glee.

"Cupcake! Where's Jasper and Willis?" he asked, looking around when the dog rolled over for belly rubs.

A homeless man with long gray hair and a sparse beard loped across the street with a big grin. "Victor, Cupcake misses you, man."

"Hey Jasper." Victor shook the man's hand then bent to pick up the small dog. "You know better than to let her run into the road."

"Yeah, yeah. She never listens to me, only Willis. He's at the clinic. Someone knocked him around for that coat you gave him."

Victor frowned and pulled out his wallet. "Go get yourself a hot meal and something for Cupcake. Tell Jasper I'll try to stop by before I head home."

"Will you be needing..." Jasper started then glanced my way for the first time. "You know."

Victor shook his head and took a step closer to me. "I'm good. This is the woman I was telling you about."

Jasper tucked Cupcake under one arm and took my hand in his. "I'm so glad he found you."

Victor cleared his throat before changing the subject. "Like I said, I'll try to stop by before we depart. Take care of yourself, Jasper."

The homeless man nodded then turned and waited for traffic to clear so he could jog back across the street. I gave Victor a questioning look but his eyes followed the man until he was safely across and disappearing around the corner.

"Was I lost?" I asked, referring to Jasper's comment.

"I think he misunderstood."

"He's not the only one. How do you know him?" I said as we continued toward the car.

He shrugged. "Joseph and I volunteered at the homeless shelter a few times."

His nonchalant response rendered me speechless. Never in a million years would I have imagined volunteering with the homeless as one of Victor's past times. When we got to the car, I hesitated then pulled my phone from my pocket—this new information and a nice buzz making me bold.

"Hi Dona. We're good but the hotel you picked is awful. There's a dozen within walking distance. I'll get us set up at a different one and let you know."

I ended the call before she could respond then pushed the little button on the side and acknowledged the shutdown notification. "Toss me the keys, we've got a while until sunrise. Let's see what this baby can do."

Victor's phone started to ring. He looked at the screen and ignored the call. "You'll get a chance to drive but not after that many drinks."

"Come on. I'm not that breakable."

He took a step closer and whispered suggestively. "I know."

I laid my hand on his chest and leaned in, brushing my lips against his. "Let's go find a hotel that isn't bugged."

Chapter Eleven

I woke about an hour before sunset. We'd used Rowan's trick with the foil to block the windows of the cheap motel room. This place was definitely not on the Immortal Council's approved list but it gave us a few more hours alone. Once again, I was feeling guilty for using him to ignore my real problems.

It was weird watching Victor sleep. He was completely motionless; he didn't even breathe. Actually, none of the reborn needed to breathe but most found it too awkward to stop, even after their death. When they were sleeping, they literally looked dead. The longer I watched, the more it creeped me out.

I pulled my suitcase into the bathroom and turned on the shower. The room quickly filled with steam, even with the fan on so I cracked the door. I washed my hair twice while I thought about what I was going to say to the Council. Tonight's meeting could change everything.

This update sounded like a book report but for my life. Had I completed all the necessary paperwork for this and for that? Had I completed the bonding ceremony with my entire clan? Last but certainly not least, what was my platform? Yes, platform, like I was running for office.

The Council wanted everyone to have a job and to make the world better. All living immortals were to have a platform. I'd gone in circles trying to find something I was passionate enough about to devote my immortality to. Once I figured out what it was, I felt pretty damn good about myself.

I was braiding my hair when Victor knocked gently on the door. He handed me my phone. I turned it on and groaned. There were twenty-five missed calls from Dona, multiple texts from her and Rowan, and another voicemail from Tom.

"I've already talked to Rowan but you'd better call Dona before she explodes."

I stepped out and heard him turn on the shower. After a few moments, I heard the curtain pull closed. Opening the missed calls, I pressed Dona's number.

"Oh my God, Arabella! Where have you been? We've been going crazy over here. Your meeting has been changed and I couldn't reach you."

"It's okay, Dona. I'm fine. My phone just died."

She paused for a moment and I swear I heard her mumble something about Victor's phone being dead too. "Your meeting was moved up from midnight to eleven. You've got less than an hour to get there."

I pinned the phone between my ear and my shoulder to put on my watch. "We aren't far, so no biggie. Any chance Rowan is nearby?"

I heard the phone being transferred. "I can't leave you alone for one minute, can I?"

"You're not my babysitter, Rowan. Any luck on that work around?"

"Nothing yet but don't let them separate you. I never liked the fact he offered to go back so quickly."

"Wait, what? Why didn't you say something before?"

"Sorry, Love. He asked me not to worry you. Keep him close. Call me when you get back to your hotel. The real hotel this time."

"Copy that."

I ended the call and angrily put on mascara. In hindsight, that was a bad idea. I stabbed myself in both the cheek and nose during the application. A few tissues and a quick swipe of lip gloss and I was ready.

Victor emerged from the bathroom a few minutes later looking so good that it almost distracted me from how mad I was at him. They hadn't requested him back; he had come with me as protection. Too bad he was the one who needed it.

"When were you going to tell me that you didn't need to come here to personally file those papers?"

He adjusted his cuffs before he answered. "You shouldn't travel alone."

"No shit but *you* didn't have to come back here. It's almost like you want the Council to kill you. Great news, our meeting got bumped. We're up in half an hour."

He stepped close, put his hands on my waist, then gave me a quick kiss. "Everything will be fine."

"Yeah, I'm sure they won't notice the lip gloss at all." I used my thumb to wipe it off then grabbed my bag. "Let's go."

I didn't believe our destination was really the temple until Victor pulled into the underground parking structure and the crossing arm lifted. He parked in a reserved spot and killed the engine.

"Follow my lead," he said as he helped me from the car.

"Don't you work for me?"

"Yes, but I've spent the last six months learning how they work." He stepped close and I was afraid he was going to kiss me in view of all the cameras. "Arabella, please."

I nodded and followed him to an elevator. He keyed in a code and it started to move. Fancy! The chime sounded making me jump. I made a point to put space between us and looked defiantly at the camera in the corner.

The lift stopped at ground level and opened to a brightly lit foyer. A dozen or so people moved about but didn't seem to be in any hurry. Victor took a left and started down a long hallway. I followed while trying to peek into the rooms we passed. We exited this building and walked across the courtyard. Trees whispered above us as we passed multiple small gardens. It was beautiful, even at night.

He keyed in another code and we entered a smaller building. This one had a fountain inside. A painting of Jesus giving baptisms hung above it. My steps slowed as I looked at the image. There was something familiar about one of the men in the painting.

"Arabella, we're going to be late," Victor called and I hurried to catch up.

He stopped outside a set of double doors, a leather briefcase in one hand. I'd been so distracted I hadn't noticed it before. My guess was it held all the paperwork we were supposed to be filing. Hadn't the Council heard of email?

Six people in robes sat at a long table. Two smaller tables sat on either side, similar to a courtroom but instead of a gallery, there were pews behind the smaller tables. A podium rose behind the table of councilmembers. My hand twitched and I felt compelled to do the sign of the cross as I entered. All those years in the Catholic church created habits that were hard to ignore.

Victor motioned toward the table on the right. We stayed standing and I wondered what was supposed to happen next. The answer would have made me roll my eyes if I hadn't been so nervous. This wasn't a book report; it was the nightmare where you show up in gym class with no pants on.

"Arabella Simon, thank you for taking time to meet with us." An Asian woman who was sitting in the middle of the group spoke. I remembered her as acting Council Leader Tsu from one of my many virtual meetings. "You may sit if you wish."

Oh, I wished. The shoes Dona packed for me were not comfortable but my last-minute flip flop addition didn't really go with the suit I was currently wearing. I don't remember buying any dress shoes since the fire so these either weren't mine or were brand new.

"Victor, you may join the others in the hall." She pointed toward the door.

Her tone indicated it wasn't an option. Rowan's suggestion to keep Victor close popped into my head. That and I wasn't going to let them boss around members of my clan. Huh? That sounded vaguely familiar.

Maybe Seraphine was on to something, or maybe she was batshit crazy. Either way, don't push my people around.

"As my legal counsel, I request that he stays." I forced my best smile.

"Very well. As acting Leader of the Immortal Council, I will be presiding over this review."

She introduced the rest of the councilmembers from left to right and I promptly forgot almost everyone's names. I'd ask Victor later. What were they going to do? Kick me out of their club? One could only hope.

"Arabella, you had a late start to your living immortal training. Do you feel you are getting the resources you need?"

"Yes. My assistant, Dona, has set aside regular time each week to review immortal history, including rules and laws. That, and my father finally delivered the chest that had been misplaced since my twelfth birthday."

There were some mutterings from the six and I snuck a glance at Victor. He had organized the papers and was taking notes on a legal pad. Very old school. I noted his very neat handwriting and my mind wandered back to his letter.

"Have you had any additions to your clan?" a very elderly looking councilmember asked.

"I have one pending request but otherwise no."

"Elaborate on pending," he said.

"I haven't decided if I'm ready to add members to my clan yet thusly, the request is pending." I tried to keep the annoyance out of my voice. Wasn't it my clan? Didn't I get to make any of my own decisions?

This was supposed to be my show so I resisted the urge to turn and look at Victor again. I needed to prove to them that I was taking my role seriously. The councilmember nodded and sat back. So far, so good.

Young was his name. Yes! Two out of six. I'd have this down in no time.

"The estate has been fully transferred into your name but will revert to the Council if circumstances arise in which you no longer need it," Tsu said.

That sounded ominous so I filed it away to ask Rowan later. Each councilmember asked me questions about my history, my clan members, or my plans. Most of the questions were straightforward and I thought I was killing it. We'd be home in no time.

"Have you decided on a platform for you and your clan?"

"I have, Councilwoman Tsu. I would like to take a stand against child trafficking. As you know, my Steward was forced to participate in his youth and it seems fitting that we approach this continuing injustice together."

More murmuring and this time it took the acting leader a few moments to quiet everyone so she could speak. She gave me a sad smile and her tone turned condescending.

"That is a very noble platform but one we must deny. You will be given an extension of..." She looked at the young Hispanic councilmember at the end of the table who was taking notes. He held up five fingers. "An extension of five months to propose a new platform."

Frustration had me leaning forward. "I don't understand. Child trafficking is a huge problem. With the Council's resources worldwide, why would my platform be denied?"

"If I may? Councilmen Imbarra." A dark-skinned man introduced himself again as if he knew I didn't remember anyone's name. "This cause has been attempted before. Now is not the time to churn those waters."

I opened my mouth to argue but Victor put his hand on my arm and leaned in to whisper in my ear. "Stop pushing. It doesn't benefit them."

The acting leader started speaking again, which kept me from calling them out on their bullshit. "Have you completed the paperwork we sent with Mr. River?"

"Yes. I mean, no. I forgot to sign the last set. Give me a second." I grabbed the power of attorney pile and scribbled my name on the forms.

When I handed them back, I whispered, "Do *not* make me regret this."

Victor gathered two copies of everything and brought them to the man taking notes. He flipped through to confirm everything was filled out properly and nodded his approval. Before Victor stepped away, he handed him a large Manilla envelope.

"To update your Steward on the ongoing rogue issue." His voice was low but I still caught the urgency in his tone.

What rogue issue? I opened my mouth to ask that very question when Imbarra stood and rested his hands on the table.

"I have one final question before we conclude this session. You've completed the binding ceremony with all your clan members, correct?"

"Yes." I held his gaze.

"Including Mr. River?"

"My Steward suggested I complete everything before I met with the Council and I have done so."

Imbarra's eyes bore into mine but I refused to look away. This man was a bully and had something to prove. Even though the idea that the Council was here to help me was being crammed down my throat, it was becoming more and more clear that I was here to help them. I could see now that Victor was not part of whatever plan they had for me. This man was not happy that he was once again in my life.

"And you approve of his sentence for the murder of your child?"

He knew just how to twist the knife in my heart. My stomach clenched and words fled my mind. I hadn't thought of it that way. Such a blunt, hurtful thing to say. I cleared my throat and pushed the pain back down.

"According to my Steward, I am not privy to the details of his punishment." I should have kept my damn mouth closed but this guy wasn't going to manipulate me. "Which I believe is wrong. Victor is a member of my clan. I have the right to know the details of his sentence."

The councilmembers looked at the acting leader and Imbarra looked like the cat who swallowed the canary. I had just stepped over the line. He was going to be a problem.

"You are not in a place to make demands on the Council!" Tsu snapped at me. "Our word is law. If you have not yet reached that part of your lessons, I suggest you review it at once. This meeting is over."

Victor motioned for me to stand as the councilmembers filed out. We waited a few moments then exited the way we came. All the people that were milling around earlier were gone. Victor wouldn't speak until we were in the car and about a block away.

"God dammit, Arabella! Why couldn't you leave it alone?"

"I have the right to know."

"Of course you do but you can't lie. Everyone on the Council knows someone told you, especially Imbarra. He's basically Chatelain's right-hand man."

"But I didn't lie. Rowan told me I wasn't allowed to know the details, which is exactly what I said."

"Listen to me. I spent the last six months watching them, learning their tells. They know you're lying. Why they let us leave is what's bothering me."

"Fine." I crossed my arms and sulked. "If you think they are up to something, then they are. Take me to the hotel but I'm not letting you out of my sight."

Chapter Twelve

I was pretty sure I had never stayed in a hotel this fancy before. The lobby was decorated in gold and cream tones while crystal chandeliers sparkled above. Despite the ridiculously late hour, someone played a grand piano to my left. Huge fresh flower displays were everywhere, filling the air with a rich aroma. My heels clicked loudly on the marble floor as we approached the registration desk.

A very attractive woman with long dark hair and hazel eyes smiled brightly as we approached. "Victor, welcome back."

"Nice to see you, Silvie. We have two rooms reserved under Simon."

Her eyes darted toward me then back to her computer screen in a quick dismissal. "I show check-in was scheduled for yesterday. Did you still need two nights?"

I stepped up. "Just one. I'd prefer adjoining suites."

She tapped the keys with her long burgundy nails and her smile was not as friendly when she made eye contact with me again. "I'm so sorry but we don't seem to have anything together at the moment."

Victor leaned in and I could feel the persuasion when he spoke. "She's my boss and I'm trying to make a good impression. Could you look one more time?"

Tapping continued and Silvie's smile soured but she held it in place. "My mistake. Looks like we have something on the eleventh floor, east side. Will that work?"

I nodded and she kept typing for what felt like an hour. My feet were screaming but this place was too nice to walk around barefoot. Plus, I was getting hungry. When she finally passed the room keys across the counter, I snagged them both.

"Are there any places nearby to eat that are still open?"

Silvie looked genuinely confused for a moment and I realized she was only used to dealing with reborn. "Our café is open twenty-four hours a day, as is room service."

"Thanks." I glanced at the room numbers, immediately forgetting what they were, and started toward the elevators.

Victor placed his hand on my lower back and led me past the main elevators to a separate one in an alcove to the left. I took a step away to create some space once inside. Between my feet, growing hunger, and how we'd left the Council meeting, I was no longer in a good mood. If I had my preference, we'd leave Utah right now. Even the freaking sun got to make decisions for me!

Once on the eleventh floor, I pulled the keys out of my pocket: 1151 and 1153. I handed the second set to Victor then stopped to ease off my shoes. It wasn't fair that even as an immortal, I still got freaking blisters! I was going to drown my sorrows in overpriced room service. Maybe they had a mini bar too.

My mood improved slightly once I saw the room. The bed was huge and looked super comfortable. Plus, it had a jacuzzi tub. That was happening immediately. After turning on the TV and finding a movie, I spied a small leather folder on the nightstand and flipped through it to find the room service menu.

A knock on my door made me jump. If it was Silvie looking to hook up with Victor, I'd probably lose it. It wasn't like Victor was mine but the surge of jealousy at her overly warm welcome bothered me more than it should have. I couldn't fault him for being with her during his time here. She was gorgeous and for all I knew Victor thought I was happily married to Tom. If he hadn't written that damn letter, I'd probably had the good sense to keep him at arm's length.

When I peeked through the peephole, no one was there. My shoulders relaxed a little but the headache and hunger continued to grow. I heard the knock again and realized it was coming from the door that attached the two suites. Oops!

I flipped the lock on my side and pulled the door open without looking. One, to hide my embarrassment. Two, because my eyes were too busy deciding between the brisket sandwich or crispy fish tacos. Screw it, I was ordering both, and there was indeed a mini bar.

"You really should be more careful," Victor scolded me.

"Don't tell me what to do. I've had enough of that tonight." I picked up the room phone then put it back down. "Do you want anything?"

He shook his head. "Leave this door unlocked. I'll be next door if you need me."

"Silvie seems nice. Do you know her well?" I didn't like how it sounded and I really hated how it made me feel.

Victor sighed and I enjoyed the fact that he couldn't say what he wanted since we both knew we were being listened to. "She works for the Council. If you need anything, call the front desk and ask for her by name. She's very good at her job."

"I bet she is." I glanced at my watch; sunrise wasn't too far off. "Guess I'll see you in a few hours."

He turned to leave but stopped at the doorway. "Stay in the hotel, please."

"There you go telling me what to do again, but whatever. I'm going to eat, take a long bath, and watch a movie. Don't worry about me."

My cell phone started ringing so I waved him off and started digging through my bag for it. I missed the call so I had to call Rowan back.

"Are you at the hotel?"

"Yes, *Dad*." I really needed to eat something. "Hey, the Council gave you something about a rogue problem. Is that something I should know about?"

There was silence on the other end and I wondered if the call had been dropped. Then, I remembered that Rowan also knew the hotel was bugged. Apparently, the rogue issue was not something I was supposed to know about. Great!

"You know what, never mind. We survived the big Council review but they seem annoyed with me. The feeling is mutual. We're at the hotel until our flight leaves tomorrow night. Everything good there?"

"Steve almost destroyed the lawn mower replacing the blade but otherwise, all is well." He hesitated. "Do I need to remind you to stay in the hotel?"

"Good Lord! You all treat me like a kindergartener. I hadn't planned on leaving but now it's starting to feel like a challenge. I can go for a walk if I damn well want to."

Rowan laughed. "Just be careful."

· · · ·

NEITHER THE FOOD NOR the bath made me feel better and I ignored the mini bar knowing I'd only end up with a hangover. Even though I was exhausted, I tossed and turned. The bed was too soft and I felt like I was being suffocated by it and life. Around noon, I gave up and headed downstairs. They told me not to leave the hotel, fine. I'd stay in the hotel but that didn't mean I had to be locked in my room.

The busy lobby made it easy to hide in plain sight. I browsed the shops inside and found myself giggling at the inflated prices until a red floral sundress that caught my eye. Without too much thought, I added it to my room bill and asked them to deliver it later. After leaving the shop, I noticed a courtyard garden.

The air was warmer than I expected after the overly air-conditioned hotel. The sun filtered through the trees creating pockets of light and shadow on the flowers. The smell was heavenly. I spotted a little marble bench and sat down to soak up some sun. Road noise tried to disturb the tranquility but after a while I was able to convince myself it was just the water bubbling in the nearby fountain.

A shadow crossed my path, making me open my eyes. Tom stood in front of me with two to-go coffee cups. For a moment, I wondered if I was dreaming.

"Hi. I saw you out here and thought you might like some?" He held out one of the cups.

I nodded and took a sip; cinnamon was the prevalent flavor. It wasn't anything I'd had before and reality came rushing back. I wasn't dreaming and no amount of wishing was going to change our reality.

"This wasn't really for me, was it?"

He sat on the bench and gave me a shy smile. "No, but I did see you and thought maybe we could talk."

I sat up and put the cup between us, treating it like some sort of cardboard shield. "Are you staying here?"

"Yeah. Tommy's at the pool."

Silence began to stretch but I didn't know where to begin. "You're happy?"

He shrugged and shook his head. "Everything happened so fast. I don't really know how to feel. What about you?"

"I'm okay." As soon as I said it, I realized it was starting to be true. "Life kind of shoved us in different directions, huh? What about Tommy and Rachel? Are they happy?"

His mouth turned up in a smile that made his eyes sparkle. "Tommy is such a great kid. I feel bad I missed so much time with him. Rachel is understandably hesitant, but she's built a good life for them both and is willing to let me be part of it. What part, we haven't really figured out yet."

"Can I give you some advice?" I asked, taking another sip when he nodded. "Tell her everything. Don't hold back because you think she won't like it or you think you're protecting her."

Tom didn't respond, just rested his elbows on his knees and looked at the ground. "You should stay away from Victor."

"About that... Why did you tell the Immortal Council about my baby? How did you even know about them in the first place?"

He turned to look at me, his expression grim. "I've known about them for a long time. Once Victor started his transition, they approached me too but I turned them down. I have no interest in immortality."

"You do realize they were going to kill him, right? I know you have your differences but he's family, your twin brother. That must mean something."

"He's poison, Arabella. I can't believe you of all people are defending him. Look at what he did to Rachel, what he did to you. He stole your future."

"He's not your problem anymore." *And neither am I*, I thought as I stood. "You knew what I was, didn't you?"

"We could've had a long happy life together. It didn't matter—"

"Until it did," I cut in. A tear slipped from the corner of my eye. Of all the things he kept from me, this was the one that really mattered. "I need to go. I wish you the best, Tom. I really do."

I kept walking through the lobby and down the street. I noticed the light rail and got on the train, not caring where it went. Two stops later, I got off and began walking again, unable to sit still. Everything was a blur through my tears.

Crowds of colors pressed against me as cars honked and zoomed past. My breaths started to come out too fast and spots pricked my already blurry vision. I needed to get away but I couldn't get away from myself. As I turned to go back the way I came, my shoulder bumped into someone and I mumbled an apology.

"Hey, are you okay?" a voice asked.

I blinked and focused on his concerned face then glanced at his companion. He seemed vaguely familiar but the guy I bumped looked like one of dozens of hipsters I'd already passed, down to the blond man-bun. Both had golden irises indicating they too were first generation vampires.

"Just having a rough day." I looked around and realized I had no idea where I was.

"We're headed to the Red Chicken Shack. Nothing cheers me up better than some spicy fried chicken. Do you want to join us? I'm Sam, this is Tyson. My girl, Jaime, is meeting us there."

I wiped the tears from my cheeks. "Arabella."

• • • •

HE WAS NOT KIDDING about the spicy chicken. It was super juicy and my lips were stinging by the time I was done. Jaime was a tiny Vietnamese gal who was training to be an MMA fighter. I liked her the moment we were introduced. We talked about self-defense maneuvers until the guys looked a bit uncomfortable.

At some point, we ended up in a nearby bar. I stuck to ginger ale but did let Sam buy us a round of shots. My phone vibrated in my pocket and I cringed when I looked at the time.

"Sorry, guys, but I've got a flight to catch. If you are ever in Montana, give me a call." I scribbled my phone number on a napkin then took one more hug from Jaime.

I stepped outside to answer my phone. "Don't be mad."

"Where are you?" Victor ground out.

I hurried to the intersection. "West Temple and 300 South?"

"Stay there." The line went dead.

A few minutes later, Victor came to a screeching stop in front of me. I opened the door and took my time getting in. When I turned to look at him, my blood ran cold.

"What?"

"I read the file about the rogue issue. They've figured out how to be out during the day."

Chapter Thirteen

"How is that even possible?" I asked as he wove in and out of traffic.

"The how doesn't matter right now. What matters is *you* need to stop putting yourself at risk."

I folded my arms across my chest. "You all seem to have forgotten that I can take care of myself. I was literally paid to protect others."

We didn't speak again until we got to the airport. He parked in a different area and headed to the rental car section. I just pulled my suitcase behind me and followed. The more I thought about it, the more I realized he was right. I had people who depended on me now.

"Welcome to Budgets," the teen girl with amazingly pink hair greeted us.

"Hi. I'm dropping off my vehicle for transport. The information is under River."

She smiled and started typing on her tablet. "I see it here. 1969 Ford Mustang, California license plates, where did you park?"

"38C." He handed her the keys.

"Oh, Montana. I went to Glacier National Park on a school trip once." She handed him the tablet to sign. "Have a nice flight. We'll take good care of your vehicle."

When we'd walked for what felt like forever, I finally asked. "You're shipping your car?"

He let out an annoyed breath. "I had planned on driving it back so we'd have some time alone but we need to get back. Now."

• • • •

I FELL ASLEEP ON THE flight and the drive to the house was short. Steve didn't let me drive this time and I didn't press it since my mind was whirling with selfish guilt. Everyone in my clan was ready and waiting when we arrived, including Eve.

We hadn't used this room much; Dona called it "The Parlor". It was right off the front door. Dona kept it for guests, not that we'd had any but I guess it was a possibility. Two of the walls were floor to ceiling windows. The furniture was delicate; ferns and orchids dominated the space. It was a good thing she had a green thumb; I killed cactus. The silence was oppressive as I found an empty chair.

Eve ran over to give me a hug and I whispered. "Let's talk after?"

She nodded and took her spot next to Acacia. Steve stood in the corner like a statue with his arms folded. Dona held her tablet at the ready. Rowan paced with his hands behind his back. Victor disappeared into the house and I wished I could have gone with him.

He returned with a ginger ale for me, handed the folder to Rowan, then took the only remaining seat. Rowan finally stopped pacing and let out a long slow breath. He opened the folder and spread the contents on the mosaic tile table in the center of the room.

"Once again, the Council ignored a problem until it became too large to hide. Rogues aren't an individual concern anymore. They have formed their own network with one goal in mind: kill all of the living immortals."

"That doesn't make any sense. Don't they need us?" I asked.

"If you believe the Council, they do, but maybe they're tired of living under all their rules too." He gave me a serious look.

"Point taken. Victor said they can be out in the sun. How is that possible?"

Rowan shook his head. "The Council haven't figured that one out yet. Any time their people get close, they don't come back."

I spread the papers over the table. There were pages of text followed by photos, lots of photos. One caught my attention; another stopped my heart. I sat back, feeling cold. My hands shook as I held a photo of Sam and Jaime.

"I know them." My voice sounded hollow and I realized my breathing was erratic. Spots appeared in my peripheral vision. I was about to pass out.

Eve hurried over and pushed my head between my legs then rubbed my back. "Take slow, deep breaths."

Once the spots faded and my heart stopped galloping in my chest, I sat back up. I made eye contact with Victor. He hadn't told them I'd left the hotel. It was time to get everyone up to speed. No more lies by omission.

I put the first picture on top. "This was one of the guys at Gambini's from girls' night a couple weeks ago. Right, Dona?"

She leaned in and gasped, confirming my suspicion. I put the photo of Sam and Jamie on top of the first. "And I just spent the entire day with these two, and another guy, Tyson. He isn't in this stack of photos but I felt like I'd seen him before too."

I sat back, folded my arms, and stared at Rowan. He looked as furious as I felt. I was lost, literally and figuratively, this afternoon and thought I had been taken in by some genuinely nice people. Now, I just felt like a fool. The Council had put me at risk by keeping me in the dark and I was tired of it all.

"Tell me everything, Rowan. Now."

I hadn't meant for my words to be a demand but as soon as they left my lips, I knew they were. I was too emotional to take it back. Everywhere I turned, I was being manipulated. I was supposed to be their clan leader. It was well past time I started acting like it.

Rowan explained that the rogues had started out as reborn immortals who had, through no fault of their own, lost their living immortal either by choice or banishment. It happened sporadically but Seraphine sped the process along during her quest for world domination. Once the reborn realized losing their living immortal didn't cause instant death, they went into hiding. After centuries alone, they started pairing up and making clans of their own. Strength in numbers made survival easier. It also allowed them to stay off the Council's radar since they could overwhelm their hit men if one was discovered.

Disgruntled clan members were recruited by the rogues. Some would fake their deaths, others would just walk away, never to be seen again. The older living immortals barely noticed until their numbers started dwindling.

The shit hit the fan when Seraphine's people were forced into new clans as part of her punishment. She had run her clan so differently and against the Council most couldn't fit in anywhere. The rogues picked them up at alarming speed. They had enough numbers now that they had started taking out the living immortals. Three had fallen so far.

There had been an attempt on Chatelain's life but it failed. That was when the Council finally started to take this problem seriously. That's why they let Victor and I leave without a fight. They had bigger fish to fry.

Too many unanswered questions remained. Why did they want all the living immortals dead? How were they able to get around the whole sun thing? Why hadn't they taken me out when they had the chance? There had to be more to this than genocide.

It was nearly sunrise by the time Rowan finished. The room had already begun to brighten. We weren't solving anything this morning but at least we knew what we were dealing with.

I stood and stretched. "Everyone go to bed. Rest and we'll regroup at sunset."

"I'll take first watch," Steve said from the corner. He'd been still so long, I'd forgotten he was there.

"First watch?" I asked.

Rowan looked defeated. "If the rogues are free to roam in the sun, you need to be protected around the clock. Steve is the oldest. He can endure the pull of sleep the easiest. The rest of us will have to learn to fight it the best we can to keep you safe."

"What about me?" Eve put her hands on her hips.

I smiled and put my arm around her. "And you. Let's go grab some snacks. We're relegated to the basement for a while."

Steve may be able to resist the pull of sleep but he was still vulnerable to the sun. He had the scars to prove it too. It wasn't fair to put him in harm's way while he was keeping me safe. Everyone made their way farther into the house but I stopped Rowan.

"I'm sorry. I didn't mean to do that."

"Ara, Love, you are finally figuring out how this all works. No harm done. I had planned on laying it all out for you anyway. I've been forced to do a whole lot worse than tell the truth. Get some sleep."

"You too."

• • • •

EVE AND I SET UP SHOP in the game room. While it was still on the first floor, the light blocked windows kept Steve safe. We had easy access to the basement from here too. I knew I'd get tired eventually but my mind was going a million miles per hour at the moment. Too much had happened in the last twenty-four hours for my tiny brain to comprehend. Plus, I needed to talk to my friend.

She went all out on the snacks: chips, cookies, crackers with sausage and cheese, and fancy stuffed olives I didn't even know we had. She even thought to grab a couple big bottles of water. Steve took up position by the door, facing outward.

"You can sit in here with us, Steve," I offered.

"Thank you, but no. Here is good."

Eve gave me a look and I couldn't help but giggle. Steve's heart was in the right place but he could be very serious. That was okay because what I wanted to talk to Eve about was serious too and it was better to not have an audience.

"Are you sure you want to become reborn?" I asked her.

She had just taken a bite of a cracker sandwich and chewed slowly as if to collect her thoughts. "Even more now."

"Even more now that there are a group of crazy people that want to murder me? Did Victor drop you on your head as a baby?"

"Very funny. Tom was actually the one who dropped me but not on my head." She handed me a cracker sandwich. "I wanted to do this for a while but something about Victor's living immortal rubbed me the wrong way. Clearly, I dodged that bullet but now I have the perfect option. Arabella, I always wanted you as family and now I can be your sister forever."

"More like my kid, but I see what you're saying. I'm going to be honest with you. I wasn't sure I wanted to grow my clan. Ever. I'm still figuring out how this world works and I don't want to force anyone into it that isn't prepared. Once again, life seems to be pushing me along faster than I want." She waited for me to continue. "If you say you're ready, then I'll grant your request."

"Oh, thank you!" She threw her arms around me and I returned the gesture. "Can we start now?"

"No time like the present. It might be weird though."

Surprisingly, it wasn't as awkward I had expected. We'd shared blood from a small cut at each other's wrist. Maybe it was because of our already close friendship, maybe it was because we both knew what was coming and the pressure of impending death wasn't a factor. Either way, the first step was done and we could both breathe a sigh of relief.

Sharing blood three times wasn't actually necessary for transition. It was all about intention. Seraphine really enjoyed the power trip of forcing her devoted to wait until she was ready—or until she forgot about them. The best part was Eve still had a long mortal life ahead of her. This just ensured if shit hit the fan here, I wasn't leaving her defenseless.

Eve tried to explain chess to me but my brain was finally winding down. After the fourth time explaining the castle moved in a straight line, I called it a night. She headed to her room and I stood in the hall with Steve a few steps behind. I couldn't go up to my rooms and I really didn't want to sleep in a chair. Guess it was time to set up some of the unused rooms for situations like this.

Out of options, I headed down to Victor's rooms. If all the secrets were being laid out on the table, Steve had a right to know there was something going on between the two of us. I didn't know what that was yet, but it *was* something. He didn't seem shocked or even bothered when I said goodnight and closed the door. I knew he would wait for me on the other side until the sun went down.

Victor was asleep when I crawled into bed. I snuggled up and he put his arm around me, pulling my back tight against his chest. My breath came out as a sigh and I was asleep in minutes. At least for that moment, I felt safe.

Chapter Fourteen

"Promise me you'll be more careful," Victor whispered into my hair. "I already told you, I'm not ready to live in a world without you."

I rolled over so I could face him. "I hadn't planned on leaving the hotel. Something happened and my feet just carried me away."

"Anything I can do to help?"

I smiled and leaned in for a quick kiss. "You already have. We should get up and see what the others are doing. We need a plan."

He pulled me tight against him. "Or we could stay here and let them deal with it."

"As nice as that sounds, I need to stop feeling sorry for myself and start being the leader the rest of them need me to be."

He chuckled. "That's what I thought you'd say."

After a quick detour to brush my hair and change my clothes, I began my search for the others. The house was quiet and the longer I searched, the more nervous I got. After checking all the rooms, even the unfinished ones, I went into full panic mode.

"Very good. Try again." Steve's voice carried from outside.

I ran around the side of the house to see him, Acacia, and Eve standing under the string of lights from Eve's birthday. The tables had long been moved back to the various porches but the lights remained. Building materials were neatly stacked against the house and I wondered if someone decided to make this a permanent space.

Steve wrapped Eve in a bear hug from behind and lifted her into the air. She slammed her head back into his face and jammed her elbow into his ribs. His grip loosened and she used her entire body weight to slam the heel of her foot onto his toes. He stumbled back and grinned.

"What's up guys?" I asked as I joined them in the circle.

"Steve is teaching us some self-defense," Acacia explained as he took up position behind her.

They repeated the lesson. This time he shifted his head to the side to avoid hers. Acacia slammed her boot into his knee, overextending it. He collapsed on top of her. She rammed her elbow into his trapezius and he rolled away. Her speed was impressive.

"Much better. Let's take a break." He jogged back to the house, rubbing his neck as he went.

"I could teach you a few things," I offered.

Eve helped Acacia to her feet. "Steve's a great teacher."

I frowned. "How do you know I'm not?"

"You're kinda bossy," Acacia said as she flexed her elbow.

"Rude." I acted shocked but it was true. "Where are Dona and Rowan?"

The girls looked at each other as if deciding whether or not to answer. The panic I'd felt earlier started to once again rise to the surface. I'd never suffered from anxiety attacks before. What was going on?

"They're on a supply run." Eve finally spoke but her voice had a weird echo quality. "Are you okay?"

I let out a shaky breath and sat down to stop the spinning. This was not good. Whatever the cause, now was not the time. I closed my eyes and took those slow deep breaths Eve suggested the night before. Once my heart rate returned to normal, I opened my eyes.

"What supplies?" I asked, ignoring her question.

The girls once again shared a look but this time Acacia spoke. "Rowan got a call about an hour ago. He grabbed Dona and they left in separate cars to get supplies. They didn't tell us what."

That sounded ominous. I got back to my feet and was annoyed at how badly my hands were shaking. What the hell? I stuffed them in my pockets and headed back into the house. The girls didn't follow.

Steve and Victor were in the kitchen. I made a beeline to the coffee maker. Maybe I was just tired? My trembling hands spilled coffee grounds everywhere and almost dropped the carafe in the sink while trying to fill it with water. Victor put his hands over mine and gently took the pot before I broke it.

"Thanks." I took a seat at the breakfast bar, feeling very weak.

"Everything will be fine." Steve patted me on the back and headed toward the front door to rejoin the girls. "We will protect you."

Victor handed me a steaming coffee mug then looked at me with concern. "Are you alright?"

I took a sip then almost sloshed coffee over the side trying to put the cup down. My heart was once again galloping in my chest and black spots threatened my vision. When I tilted my head up to answer, the darkness won.

• • • •

"WHAT DO YOU MEAN SHE was poisoned? When? How?" Victor yelled.

"Clearly on her little solo jaunt in the city," Rowan snapped. "Maybe if you'd watched her more closely..."

I let out a sigh and opened my eyes. The room spun and my stomach clenched. They continued to argue but my heart was pounding in my ears so I couldn't hear them clearly. The rogues had poisoned me. I had been so confused as to why they hadn't tried to take me out that the idea they had actually succeeded never crossed my mind.

A new panic rose as my mind cleared. I tried to sit up and multiple sets of hands pushed me back down.

"Ara, you need to rest," Rowan said softly.

"Where's Eve?" My voice sounded like it was in a tunnel.

"Steve worked the girls pretty hard. She went to bed," Victor answered.

My eyes finally focused on his and tears threatened to overflow. "She took my blood last night. If I was poisoned..."

I didn't have to finish. He dashed from the room and tears streamed down my cheeks. Rowan carefully picked me up in his arms and followed Victor. His steps were slow and I wanted nothing more than to run.

"You'll be fine, Ara. You've had both Victor's and my blood. The poison should burn off soon."

While his words were soothing, they were not what I wanted. I needed to hear that Eve was alright. When I heard Victor shouting her name, Rowan's feet slowed to a stop. Acacia shoved passed us with a confused look and ran toward Eve's room. Her devastated shriek confirmed my fears.

"Put me down, Rowan."

He hesitated then gently set me on my feet. My legs wobbled but he kept a grip on my elbow to steady me. The world tipped on its side for a second. I took a step but he held fast.

"I'm going with or without you," I warned.

He let go and I used the wall for support. The noise had stopped by the time I reached Eve's room. Victor was standing near the bed and I could see Acacia's legs and feet where she was laying on it. The sound of her sobs broke my heart.

When Victor turned, I saw Acacia holding Eve in her arms. Eve was completely motionless, lips slightly blue. My sister looked up at me and I've never seen such loathing. The weight of it all broke me and I collapsed to the floor.

Victor hurried to my side but I shoved him away and crawled toward the bed. I lifted my hand toward Eve's face but Acacia slapped it away. She shifted her body so they were both out of reach.

"I was trying to protect her," I sobbed.

"Get out," Acacia growled at me. I tried to speak again but she just screamed. "You did this! Get out! Get out!"

Victor scooped me up and I was in my rooms before I knew it. He set me on my bed. I rolled away and bawled into my pillow. He sat beside me but didn't move. I knew I should be comforting him—he'd just lost his sister—but my pain was too much. I couldn't take any more.

Sometime later, I heard the door creak. I wiped my eyes with my hands and sat up. The dizziness was already passing. Rowan stood across the room and waited for me to speak.

"Tell me she's going to turn. Tell me she's going to be okay." The last word came out in a broken sob.

He looked down and put his hands in his pockets before answering. "I can't tell you what I don't know."

Victor stood and quickly left the room without looking back. I'd finally come to terms with being a monster and suddenly, I was rethinking that progress. If I had just waited, Eve would still be alive and I might be dead. That was a trade I'd make in a second. My clan would find new homes. They didn't need me.

"You don't need me," I whispered as I realized it was true.

"Ara, that's not..." Rowan started.

I shook my head. "No, I mean, the rogues are right. I just murdered my best friend and would have died without reborn blood. None of you need us. We need you but you don't need living immortals to survive."

Rowan sat and looked at his clasped hands. He knew I was right. Living immortals couldn't survive without reborn blood, not long-term anyway. Would my mistake with Eve's transition break my clan's trust in me? Other than Council law, there was no reason for my clan members to stay. They could all leave. They *should* all leave.

"Now isn't the time for this discussion." Rowan looked up at me. "We need to stand together. No one is here because they are being forced. We chose to join your clan, Ara. We're here because we see something different in you."

"Raging ineptitude?"

He chuckled. "Sparkling wit. But seriously, no one is going anywhere."

My thoughts went back to Acacia's expression when I entered Eve's room and I wasn't so sure. Eve had to turn. If she didn't, everything was going to fall apart, including me.

· · · ·

JOSEPH HAD BEEN THE call Rowan received earlier. The rogues had used a slow acting poison on Chatelain, so it was likely that was what they had done to me as well. This explained my light-headedness and panic attacks after my brief interaction with them. Once I'd had reborn blood, those symptoms had disappeared.

Joseph and Rowan came up with the idea to lock me in the house for my own safety. Dona had the foresight to set me up in a temporary room until the rogue issue was under control—or at least better understood. The air mattress and mini fridge had been part of the supply run. Food had been as well, but I was too angry to be hungry.

Dona helped me inflate the bed just before sunrise. I was on the second basement level between her and Steve's rooms. Despite everything that had happened, the consensus was that I still needed around the clock protection, which meant my rooms and the main level were off limits during the day.

Rowan deposited the Council chest in an empty corner of my temporary room and set the envelope containing the rogue intel on top. I'd planned on spending a good chunk of the day scouring everything. My phone was once again dead but was plugged in to charge. I doubted there would be much help on the internet but it couldn't hurt.

A decently comfortable chair had been moved from somewhere in the house and I'd grabbed my pillows, a change of clothes, and both my hair and toothbrush. That would be everything I needed for now. I hadn't seen Acacia or Victor all night. They needed their space and right now, so did I. All we could do was wait.

"I'll be just outside if you need anything," Dona said, checking everything one more time.

My security training was kicking in. The single way in was easy to defend but the one way out was a problem. Let's not get started on the fire code violations in this house. If any of us got overwhelmed in the lower levels, there was nowhere for us to retreat or an alternate exit to use. If Eve didn't wake up tonight, I wasn't sure I'd fight the rogues if they did come.

I shook my head. The guilt that filled my mind was not helpful. I'd meant what I said to Victor about being the leader my clan needed. Time to step up. My phone beeped and I welcomed the distraction until I saw who sent the message.

I was tempted to delete Tom's text but I opened it anyway. *Eve's not answering her phone. Is she okay?*

I started typing: *She's not feeling well.*

Backspace: *She must be busy.*

Backspace again: *She's sleeping.*

I hit send then chewed my bottom lip. Had Victor told him what I'd done? He said they weren't speaking but this wasn't a normal circumstance. I thought I had closed this chapter of my life yet here it was again. The reply bubbles went on forever and I almost put away the phone, not wanting to read his reply.

Okay. I'm sorry I bothered you. I'm sorry for how we left things. I'm sorry for a lot.

I read and re-read the text. There wasn't any reason to reply and I didn't know what else there was to say. I set the phone aside and opened the chest. My personal life could wait.

Everything was how I'd left it but this time I didn't skim. Each book had a purpose and I needed to get with the program. The more I read, the more I realized it was mostly propaganda. The Immortal Council was good at it too. They phrased everything so carefully but if I really paid attention there were contradictions and gaps.

Their entire reason for being was to make the world better for living immortals, which coincidentally made up the entirety of the Immortal Council. For someone brainwashed into this from birth, it sounded like heaven. At nearly thirty and spending most of those years protecting and doing for others, it felt like entitlement to me. I wanted none of it.

They had wrapped me up in a fancy house, warm welcomes, and nearly unlimited funds so I hadn't looked too closely. I'd been so focused on myself that I was blinded by their "generosity" in a time when I felt I had lost everything. I'd sold my soul for the chance to belong to anything. My dad was right. I should have told them all to shove it.

Hours later, I put yet another book aside and moved to the floor. The rogue folder was thick. I divided the contents and started reading. The Council had known about the rogue clans for decades and done nothing other than observe. So much for the instant death sentence. Maybe that was why they let Victor leave. They wanted to watch and get as much damning information on him as they could before they struck the final blow. Well, they'd have to go through me first. His sentence was just another bullshit way to try to control me.

The Council had pretty much determined the entire rogue community was run by two men. One was Sam. The other they only had a blurry picture and no name. *How helpful!* I spent time really looking at the photos and studying what made each rogue unique. At some point, I wished for Victor's legal pad but had to make do with the Notes app on my phone.

There weren't many similarities. It appeared there were more males than females but I didn't know if that was because that ratio held true for all reborn or just rogues. They were every ethnicity, age, size, shape, etc. Their previous clans were listed when discovered but most didn't have any known affiliation. Nothing stood out except they were tired of the Council's rules.

I had spread out several dozen pictures and was about to give up when I did notice something. Sam and Jaime's photos were included in my research. It still stung that I'd been tricked so easily. But the next row of photos confirmed my suspicions.

"Dona?" I peeked out the door.

She was sitting on a folding chair with her tablet in her lap but looked up when I opened the door. One earbud was in her ear and I realized she was watching a movie. Everyone was getting some security training tonight whether they liked it or not.

"I need you to look something up for me."

She quickly stuffed her earbuds in her pocket and joined me in my room. We did leave the door open but still this was not ideal. Unfortunately, clan numbers limited our options. With all living immortals on high alert due to the rogue attacks, I doubted we could request reinforcements. I didn't really want strangers in my house right now either. Too easy for the Council to send spies rather than actual security help.

"Do you have photos of all the current living immortals?"

Her fingers danced across the screen then turned it in my direction. I scrolled through everyone until I reached my photo. None of them had gold eyes. Over a hundred total of us, spaced over centuries, and I was the only first-generation living immortal.

"Is there a regulation against first generations becoming reborn? Seraphine mentioned it but I haven't seen anything concrete."

She took the tablet back and started searching. My phone chimed but I ignored it. Her expression grew frustrated the longer she searched.

"I'm not finding anything, but I know it's here somewhere," she said with annoyance.

"Keep looking," I said as my phone chimed again.

After the third chime, I went over and picked it up. The number wasn't one I recognized and it wasn't in my contacts. If the first word hadn't been my name, I would have deleted the entire thread.

Arabella! You told us to reach out if we ever made it to Montana. If you are feeling up to company, let me know. This is Jaime, BTW. <3

I just stared at my phone then back to Dona who was still typing and scrolling, typing and scrolling. My watch started beeping and I knew sunset was approaching. Everyone needed to get up now. Our time had just run out.

Chapter Fifteen

"This is so strange. I've seen the statute. I know I have, but it's just not here." Dona was shaking her head at her tablet.

"Keep looking. I need to start rounding everyone up." I stuffed my phone in my back pocket and stepped out the door.

"Wait!" Dona hurried after me. "I'm supposed to stay with you until Rowan wakes up."

"Looks like that's our first stop then."

Rowan and Steve were awake as soon as I knocked on their doors. I sent the latter to get Victor and Acacia. It was a chicken move but we needed to have a plan that involved all of us. As much as I wanted to focus on what was going on inside the clan, the outside was coming whether we were ready or not.

We once again found ourselves in the parlor. It had the best view of the outside so we'd see if anyone came down the driveway. I flipped on all the outside lights and was impressed with how much coverage we had. No one was sneaking up on us, at least not from the front of the property. While I waited for everyone to get settled, I laid out half a dozen photos and opened the Notes app on my phone.

We waited over forty minutes before Victor showed up. "Your sister's not coming."

I nodded but wasn't surprised. The clan was not Acacia's priority right now. We'd bring her up to speed when she was ready. I wanted desperately to ask about Eve but Victor sat without another word, his focus on a brightly colored plant I couldn't identify rather than on me.

I took a deep breath to clear my thoughts. "I spent the entire day trying to figure out why the Council created this problem."

Dona gasped at my choice of words but at this point, that was how I saw it. There was no solid reason for reborn to stay attached to their living immortal other than it was their tradition that eventually turned into law. The Council has done next to nothing to support the reborn other than limit their actions and on occasion, given them housing.

"I realized yesterday that none of you need me, or more specifically reborn don't need their living immortal after the transition is complete. We, however, depend on the reborn to survive. The Council has twisted this idea until those two statements mean the same thing."

"Ara, this isn't helpful," Rowan warned.

I held up my phone. "Like the idiot I am, I gave the rogues my phone number. Guess what? They're here and would love to come visit."

Rowan closed his eyes and shook his head in disappointment. Steve looked resolute; Dona looked terrified. Victor, well he looked like Victor so I quickly glanced away. I wished Acacia and Eve were here. They'd be on my side. My eyes flicked toward the door and once again I longed to be at Eve's bedside. Unfortunately, it was time to do what was right, not what I wanted.

"What are we going to do?" Dona asked in a small voice.

"Did you find that statute?" I asked her and she shook her head so I pointed to the photos. "Victor, you dug through the Council laws. Did you find anything against turning first generations?"

Rowan picked up one of the photos and I saw the light go off. "Bloody brilliant. Ara, you're a genius."

Victor didn't seem to share his enthusiasm. "Nothing specific, no."

"Dona, pull up the photos of the living immortals and pass them around."

"First generation. That's the key. I'm the only one, or I should say, I'm the only one listed." I slapped the blurry image of the second rogue leader on the table. "I bet he's another."

"And you think that's why they can be out during the day?" Rowan was catching on quick.

"There's only one way to find out, but we have to wait until morning." I took a deep breath and continued, "I think the reason the statute is missing is because someone on the Council is helping the rogues or hindering the living immortals in a roundabout way. Unless Acacia was an anomaly, there doesn't seem to be a legitimate reason to exclude first generations from becoming reborn. I'm sure if the law does exist, someone who came to the same conclusions as I have, deleted it. That's also why there's missing information, like who Blurry Man is."

The weight of staying up for almost twenty-four hours slammed into me. I found a chair and sank into it. My eyes drifted to the doorway again while everyone talked about the discoveries amongst themselves. Plans were being developed and I did my best to listen.

My eyes closed and when I opened them, I noticed Victor was gone. They closed again and I knew I couldn't fight it any longer. I got to my feet and headed to the door. Conversation stopped.

"I need to sleep. Bring me up to speed in a few hours."

I didn't wait for a response. My feet carried me downstairs and I found myself near Eve's room. Acacia and Victor were speaking in low voices. I held my breath and tried to listen.

"But why hasn't she woken up yet?" Acacia asked.

"I don't know but this is a start. There's no one more stubborn than Eve when it comes to something she wants, except maybe your sister. If anyone can fight through this, it's her."

I smiled at his comment because it was true. Once I made up my mind about something, there was nothing that could stop me. Right now, I wanted to see Eve more than anything in the world.

That being said, I stopped just outside the door and watched them for a moment. Eve was on her back, covers pulled neatly around her, looking like a modern-day Sleeping Beauty. Her chest moved up and down like she was in a deep sleep. A sob broke through my lips and both their gazes snapped to me. Acacia looked away immediately. Victor stood and stalked my way.

He kept coming so I stepped backward until my back bumped against the wall. He held my gaze as he quietly closed the door behind him. His expression was impossible to read.

"I thought I was protecting her. I'm so sorry." My quiet voice echoed in the empty hallway.

His shoulders finally dropped and he let out a breath. "She's showing signs of transition but she hasn't woken up yet. That's not completely uncommon but we don't know what the lingering effects of the poison may be."

The silence began to stretch and I longed to hug both him and Acacia but they weren't ready. They needed their Eve back and I was the one who stole her from them. An apology was not strong enough. Only time would fix this.

I turned to go but he spoke again with a little more warmth in his tone. "I'll let you know if there are any changes."

I spun back around and wrapped my arms around him for a split second then turned and ran down the hall before he could return the hug, or not. I wasn't ready to know which yet.

• • • •

MY GENERIC RINGTONE woke me several hours later. I'd sunk into the middle of the slowly deflating air mattress and had to flail like a fish to get off of it. I knew air mattresses sucked but you can usually get a few uses before they start to deflate regularly. A better bed was on the to-do list for today.

It wasn't a number I recognized but answered anyway. "Hello?"

"Arabella, it's so nice to hear your voice."

I smiled and rolled onto the floor with a thud. This bed was evil. "You too, Lucian."

"I wanted to talk to you about your accounts. Is now a good time?"

I glanced at my watch, which read 5:39AM. "As good a time as any."

"Victor and Eve aren't answering their phones so I wasn't sure. I didn't want to bother you but I needed to ask about a recurring transfer."

I tried to ignore his comment about Eve but my chest tightened automatically. "I'm not sure I can help. My assistant has been taking care of the bills since this all started. She's really organized. I'm sure she can tell us immediately what it is."

There was a moment of hesitation and my sleep fogged brain began to clear. He was calling because there was a problem, a *recurring* problem. A sense of foreboding settled into my already tense shoulders.

"There's a five thousand dollar transfer each month. The deposits rotate between three receiving accounts but the transfer date is always the same. All the other transfers and deposits have notes attached. This one does not."

"Okay. Can you tell if this is a personal or business account?" I was trying to think of any innocent reason for these transfers. Maybe she was donating to charities?

"It's not clear," he started, then added, "If the pattern continues, the next deposit will go through on Monday."

"Got it. I'll talk to Dona and get back to you. We're dealing with a small crisis at the moment. If you don't hear from me by Sunday night, can you freeze the transfer?"

"Of course." He let out a breath. "Now that business is handled, how are you holding up?"

"It's been some year."

"That's an understatement. I expected to have a new daughter-in-law by now. Any chance that might still happen?"

"Um…" was my brilliant response, wondering if he too somehow knew something was going on between Victor and me.

He continued without pressing, "You know you are always welcome to visit if you need a break. My kids seem to adore you, as do I. I'm sure my wife will come around eventually."

Don't bet on it. "I know this is a weird question, but did you know? I mean about what I was?"

"No, Arabella, I just knew you were special."

I smiled again. "Thanks, Lucian. I'll be in touch soon."

After disconnecting, I checked and saw there was another message from Jamie. It was just a bunch of question marks, probably wondering why I never answered. She seemed like a smart woman; she'd figure it out.

I ran a brush through my hair and headed upstairs. Rowan was slumped just outside my door and looked exhausted. Actually, he looked asleep. I rolled my eyes and gently kicked his chair.

"I need to talk to Dona."

He yawned and stretched. "She went to find some donors."

"By herself? It's nearly sunrise."

"Of course not. No one is going to be alone for a while. What did you need?" he asked with another yawn.

I ignored his question. "Donors? Like humans?" My brain finally caught up. "For Eve? Can I see her?"

He grabbed my arm when I turned to run upstairs. "She's not fit for visitors. The poison must have burned through her reserves quicker than normal. She's currently being restrained until we can get her blood."

"I need to see her." My voice was darker than I intended but it did the job.

He reluctantly let go. "It's not pretty but I guess you're right."

I could hear her well before we made it to the first floor. Guttural screams followed by frantic pleading echoed down the hall. My heart broke at the sound but it also gave me hope. Even though Rowan had warned me, I was not prepared for the scene before me.

Eve's normally spotless room looked like it had been hit by a tornado. The bed was ripped to shreds and her broken dresser was on its side, contents spilling out. Eve's color was beyond pale, almost translucent. Her frantic eyes scanned the room as if she had no idea where she was. Dark red marks covered her arms, chest, and legs like she had been clawing at her skin. Acacia was sitting behind her, arms and legs tightly wrapped around her girlfriend's body, holding on for dear life. Victor blocked the doorway since the door was half off its hinges.

Both were covered in scratches and bruises. Three long fingernail scrapes ran down the side of Victor's face. His wrist was wrapped in part of his shirt. I could smell the blood, but reborn blood wasn't what she needed.

"Arabella! I'm so glad you're here." Eve's voice was hysterical. "You need to make them let me go. I'm fine. This is fine. I just need something to drink. Tell them."

I pursed my lips and stood beside Victor. At first, I'd been upset he hadn't told me the second she woke up. Now, I understood why he wouldn't leave her. My hand brushed his and I lingered for one second before I stepped forward. I was relieved when he pressed into me rather than shifting away. The show of support lifted some of the weight from my shoulders.

I spoke in quiet, even tones. "Eve, honey. We're getting you something to drink. You need to relax."

She collapsed in on herself and broke into body wracking sobs. "I can't wait. Why are you all so mean? Why do you want me to keep hurting?"

The wait was excruciating but none of us were willing to leave. Eve swung between bouts of verbal abuse and complete meltdown. The minutes ticked by and I was starting to wonder if Dona and Steve had to seek shelter rather than return. The sun was coming up. If they didn't return soon, I'd have to go out on my own to find something for Eve. There was no way she could wait until nightfall.

I heard the front door slam and I prayed it was Dona and Steve. If the rogues showed up now, we were royally screwed. Or maybe, we could release Eve on them to buy some time, despite her pale complexion and frail appearance. Both Acacia and Victor were proof of her motivation and how ridiculously strong she currently was.

Dona rushed in with a large canvas bag. "I ran out of time. The best I could do was the blood bank. We made a large financial donation. Sorry, I didn't have time to get your approval."

I nodded and put that away for when we spoke later. Maybe my bad feeling was unfounded. She'd never given me a reason not to trust her. There had to be a simple explanation for the recurring transfers.

Victor put his hand on my shoulder. "We've got this."

I nodded and hated what I did next. "Acacia, I need you to come with me."

"I am *not* leaving her." Her voice dripped with venom and she wouldn't look at me.

Rowan came into the room and stood beside Victor. "Acacia, you are the only one who can do this. I promise we'll take good care of her until you get back."

She looked up at him and I flinched at the power of her glare. "I said, I'm not leaving."

He looked at me and I knew what I had to do. Victor must have guessed my next move too because he moved to take Acacia's spot holding Eve while Rowan blocked the door.

"What are you doing? I'm not letting her go." Acacia shifted away from him but tightened her grip on Eve.

"Acacia." My tone made her look up. "You need to come with me right now."

If I thought I saw hatred yesterday, it was nothing compared to the look she gave me in this moment. I had told her I would never make her do anything she didn't want, yet here I was breaking that promise. This was for the good of my clan. She'd forgive me one day. I hoped.

As soon as her grip loosened, Eve lurched toward the door. Rowan and Victor grabbed her but she twisted and head-butted Rowan in the face. He lost his grip and fell back. Victor had a hold of one of her arms and she slashed at him with her free hand. Fingernails connected with his chest and he hissed in pain. He recovered quickly and got her arms pinned to her sides and pushed her into a sitting position on the bed. She screamed and cried. Dona approached with her bag.

I turned and walked from the room. Acacia followed two steps behind.

"I hate you," she said through gritted teeth.

"Oh yeah? I hate me too."

Early morning air rushed in when I pulled the front door open. The sun had just started to peek through the trees. Her steps faltered but she couldn't stop until I released her. I took half a dozen steps out and turned to face her.

"What are you doing?" Her voice was panicked.

"It's okay. Just one step outside."

"Have you lost your mind?" she screamed then asked, "Are you punishing me?"

I shook my head and wrapped my arms around my stomach. Please let me be right. If I wasn't, she would never forgive me. Acacia took one step out the door then another. She stopped in a pool of direct sunlight and just stood there in shock.

My breath came out in a shaky sigh. As the seconds ticked by the only sound were morning birds and the leaves rustling in the gentle breeze. She looked down at her body then back at me. Without prompting, she took another step and turned in a circle.

"How is this possible?" She continued to look at her arms and hands in the sunlight.

"You missed a lot yesterday. Let's get Eve taken care of and I'll bring you both up to speed. You can go back now."

She didn't have to be told twice; she turned and ran back into the house. Experiment one was a success. The next step would be harder and could possibly bring everything crashing down on us.

Chapter Sixteen

E ve drained all seven blood bags Dona had retrieved from the blood bank then crashed hard. Or so I was told. Acacia kicked everyone out and locked the door. The rest of the clan had gone to bed with the sun, except Victor and he was struggling.

It was just after noon and we were sitting across from each other near the stairs that lead to the second lower level. I'd grabbed a deck of cards earlier and we were attempting to play Rummy. Since I'd never played before, he kept having to explain the rules, which was my way of keeping him awake.

Personally, I thought the whole round the clock security thing was ridiculous at this point. None of them had any training and being a zombie wasn't really helpful. Steve seemed to be the only one able to stay awake and focused during the day but even he needed a break eventually.

"Let me see what you have." Victor yawned.

I tried to hide my smile as I showed my cards: Three sixes, four fours, a Queen, a one, and a seven.

"Not bad, not great," he said as he laid out his cards.

After snagging my Queen and seven, he tried to write down the score. Twice he scribbled out the number then finally threw the pen in frustration.

"I can't even add. How the hell am I supposed to protect you?"

"You're not. You're just keeping me company." I gathered up the cards and started shuffling them. Maybe we could play Go Fish.

"I need to apologize to you," he said quietly.

I kept shuffling. "No, you don't."

He reached over and stilled my hands, which made me look up into his earnest blue eyes. "Yes, I do. When Rowan told me you were poisoned, I thought I was going to lose you and it would be my fault, again. When I realized I never had you to begin with, I got angry. Old habits are hard to break."

I looked away at his admission. "Oh. I thought you meant about Eve."

"No, I'm still mad about that. I told you from the start not to change her but you just don't listen."

"I'll take that one, but the other wasn't your fault either." I started dealing us each six cards. "I know I don't listen but I'm trying. I shouldn't have left the hotel but I was upset and not thinking about anyone but myself."

He picked up the cards when I did, not knowing the game and clearly not caring. "About the Council review?"

"Do you have a four?" I asked, avoiding his question. When he just looked at me, I gave in. "I talked to Tom in the hotel garden. It didn't go well but it was long overdue."

"I'm sorry." He handed me a four and drew a new card.

His response was not what I expected. "Why are you sorry? I figured you'd be relieved."

He put his cards down and looked at me. "I'm sorry because it hurts you. I'm sorry because everything I've done to try to make your life better ends up hurting you."

"Aren't we a pair of pity-partiers? Listen, you don't get to take all the blame. Neither one of us expected to end up here," I motioned around the empty hall then continued, "playing Go Fish and hiding from the sun. I've spent the last six months feeling sorry for myself rather than moving on with what I've been given. I just started living again and I'm not going to stop because the group of psychos are gunning for me. Do you have a six?"

His lips twitched in a grin. "It's not your turn. Do *you* have a six?"

I grumbled and handed him the card. We played through the deck and well into the next before he continued the conversation.

"What does that mean for us?" he asked, keeping his eyes on his cards.

"Honestly, I don't know." I drew a card to help gather my thoughts. "You're part of my clan but I guess you could leave if you wanted."

"Is that what you want?"

"No," I said softly then hesitated because I didn't want to hurt him. "I don't want you to leave but I don't know what to do about us either. You are the only person who accepts me for who I was before and who I am now, without openly asking for something in return. I need that because I feel so fucking used and alone, but I won't continue to put your life at risk for my own selfish reasons."

He moved so we were sitting side by side and wrapped his arm around my lower back, pulling me close. "You're not forcing me to do anything I don't want and I think I've made it clear how I feel about you."

"Yeah, all six pages of it." I bumped him playfully with my shoulder.

"In my defense, I did think I was about to die. But it was all true, and you needed to hear it." He leaned over and kissed the side of my head. "We literally have an eternity to figure this out. I'm not in any hurry."

"Thank you," I said, and really meant it.

I tilted my body and gave him a peck on the lips then another. Soon after, I was straddling his lap and my shirt was halfway down the stairs. I guess this was one way to keep him awake but neither of us were paying attention to anything else.

Halfway down the hall, Eve's door crashed open and I had enough time to see her blonde head as it disappeared around the corner. She was running upstairs! I knew it was still mid-afternoon, but I didn't know what would happen if she got outside.

"Eve, stop!" I screamed and bolted after her.

Acacia was still out cold when I passed Eve's room and I picked up the pace. When I heard her fumbling with the locks on the front door,

I knew I wasn't fast enough. I made it around the bend when she threw open the door and ran out the door into the sunshine.

"No!" Victor yelled but skidded to a halt before he stepped into a pool of sunlight from the window.

I didn't hesitate and sprinted after her. She'd made it halfway up the driveway before I tackled her. Her elbow connected with my gut and all the air was driven out of my lungs. I adjusted my arm so it was under her chin and squeezed. If I could get her to pass out, I could get her back inside. Could I choke out a reborn? Fuck! They didn't need to breathe.

Eve continued to fight and I was so thrilled that she'd had a long night of defense training before her rebirth. She countered everything I attempted. What the hell had Steve taught them and how was she remembering everything so well? Wasn't there supposed to be a big black hole to erase the memory of death? I guess Eve missed that memo because honestly, she was kicking my ass.

When we were finally standing face to face, I whispered an apology and smashed my forehead into hers. She dropped like a stone and I tried to blink away the double vision but my knees went out instead. I landed on the ground next to her and kept a firm grip on her arm in case she recovered faster than I did.

We lay on the sun dappled dirt as the world spun, her in pajamas, me in my bra and shorts. Thank goodness I lived in the middle of nowhere. If that had happened outside my old house, we'd have ended up on the news or at least on someone's social media stream. My heart was racing and my breath came out in gasps; she was motionless. When I touched my forehead, it came away wet and I knew I'd cut it open. Great.

I hadn't planned on testing her sun tolerance quite so quickly but she passed. Boy, she'd passed and then some. Eve was ridiculously strong for someone who currently looked so frail but she clearly had a goal. I understood now why the Council kept newborns contained. Acacia's smooth transition must have been an anomaly.

Once my heart slowed and double vision was somewhat tolerable, I grabbed her under the armpits and dragged her back to the house. Victor was pacing in the exact same spot, hair disheveled like he'd been running his hands through it with frustration. When he saw that Eve was not burned alive, he stepped forward and instantly his hand was covered in what looked like third degree burns.

"Eve passed test two with flying colors but it looks like number three is a failure," I said and got Eve far enough into the house that we were all out of the direct path of the sun. "I was wrong. You do need me and I don't think the rogues want me dead. They want me to join their cause."

• • • •

WHEN I EXPLAINED MY afternoon adventure with Eve, Rowan and Acacia had freaked out. Both started yelling and telling me everything I was doing wrong. While I didn't disagree, I didn't have the patience to deal with them. Even after a quick sip from Victor, my head still ached from the headbutt that nearly knocked out both Eve and myself. Victor had spent the rest of the afternoon and evening keeping Eve contained as her desperation for more blood fogged her brain. I needed a minute out of the house before I exploded in frustration.

Steve and I had gone back to the blood bank to make another quick donation and withdrawal for Eve and Victor. Since neither could get sick, they were more than happy to donate any blood that couldn't otherwise be used for transfusions. I made an under the counter agreement with them so we wouldn't have to negotiate every time we had a blood emergency. Not that I was hoping for regular emergencies but a contingency seemed like a good plan.

After several more blood bags, Eve seemed to finally be getting past the frenzied blood rage and was sitting with Acacia in the game room.

Her knee bounced but Acacia held onto her hand like a vise in case she tried to bolt again. Victor's hand was still red but the blisters were gone.

"Why was Eve unaffected by the sun while Victor burned?" Rowan asked once we were all back together.

"I have two theories." I was pacing because my brain was moving too fast to sit. "One option is only reborn that I turn are safe from the sun. This explains why both Acacia and Eve were fine but not Victor. The other is the reborn need to have had my blood recently and the effects wear off over time, which could explain Eve but not Acacia nor Victor. Not all of the rogues are first generations, or were turned by Blurry Man, but we have photos of them in the sun. Therefore, I'm leaning more toward option two but I know something about first generations is important. Why else would the rogues have so damn many?"

Rowan gave Victor a sideways glance. "I'm inclined to agree with the second option as well. You and I both know Victor was never really bound to Seraphine but there is a slight chance we're wrong. Acacia is a first generation and that seems to be an important part of this process. You'll need to run another test with one of us remaining three who aren't."

Steve stepped forward. "I volunteer."

I walked over and gave his arm a sympathetic squeeze before facing the group. "Actually, I think we've run out of time. The rogues aren't going to wait for an invitation. When the sun comes up in a couple hours, we're all going to step outside."

Dona put down her tablet and gaped at me. "*I'm* not going outside. I've witnessed reborns burning to death in the sun. I won't do it."

"Dona, we need to know what we're dealing with so we can use it to our advantage. The Council hasn't figured out how the rogues are resistant to the sun. Either they're lying, which is entirely possible, or we have knowledge the rogues don't know we have. We are all in this together," Rowan explained.

"I'm not doing it." She turned her face from the group and started typing.

I walked over and glanced at the tablet then pulled it from her lap. "Seriously? You're going to report me rather than have a discussion? Dona, I'm not going to throw you out the door and lock it behind you. We're going to be as safe as we can. If it makes you feel better, you can go last."

She looked around the room desperately trying to find someone on her side but found nothing but resolute faces. My clan was standing behind me and she was outnumbered. Her hesitation made me once again wonder if she was hiding something. But I too had seen what happened to reborns in the sun.

Her eyes met mine. "Fine, but if anyone even ends up with even a sunburn, I'm reporting you."

"Dona, if anyone gets a sunburn, I'll report myself," I said and handed her tablet back.

Chapter Seventeen

By six in the morning, everyone had taken my blood again. My head ached just like the few times I'd donated blood in college, making me realize this was not something I could do on a regular basis. I had no clue if my idea would work or if this experiment would just weaken half my support, and me in the process. The rogues were going to show up any minute. I could feel it. House tension was at an all-time high.

Hand in hand, Eve and Acacia followed close behind me as I made my way to the main level. My sister had refused to leave her side even though the old Eve was starting to make a comeback. Steve and Victor were next, followed by Rowan and finally Dona. She'd donned long sleeves, a skirt that went to her ankles, and a floppy sun hat as secondary protection.

Acacia, Eve, and I stepped out the front door and walked about twenty feet before turning around. The early morning sun blended through the leaves creating shards of light and dark. No sound came from the house.

"Steve, are you ready?" I called.

He didn't answer but strode with purpose out the door and all the way to us. He looked pained but the strain faded as he turned his face upward into the light. His eyes closed and a sense of peace washed over his features that I had never seen. The tension in my shoulders eased a fraction. One down.

"Victor, your turn."

There was an understandable delay after his reaction yesterday and for a moment, I thought maybe he hadn't heard me. He appeared, walking slowly, and stopped at the door frame. His gaze fell on each of us then he took the remaining steps to stand beside me.

"Are you okay?" I whispered.

"Yes and no, but we can talk about it later."

"Rowan? Dona? So far so good. You're up," I called toward the house.

They were to be the last after I determined the rest were okay. I heard shuffling and I knew Rowan was half dragging Dona out. That had been the plan in case she changed her mind and refused to come out on her own. Rowan was fairly confident that everything would be fine but she was still fighting every step.

Once they were both outside, her body relaxed. She lifted her hand into the sunshine and turned it this way and that. After a moment, she took off her hat and lifted her face to the sun like Steve had. It was then that I realized I had no idea how old she was or how long it had been since she'd seen the sun's light.

"Okay." Rowan clapped his hands together. "I think that's enough for today."

Apparently, his bravado had been all show. He really knew how to have my back and I appreciated it more each day. While everyone survived without any damage, he didn't want to risk being out too long and was the first one back into the house. The rest followed reluctantly after. Soon, it was just Victor and me standing alone.

"It's later. What's up?"

Victor moved so he was back in the direct path of the sun. "I never thought I'd miss the sun until it was gone."

I wrapped my arms around his neck and gave him a squeeze. "Now you don't have to miss anything."

He put his hands on my waist and pulled me to him for a quick kiss. "You never cease to surprise me with how amazing you are."

The sound of a photo being snapped jerked me away from Victor. There were four people standing in the driveway: Sam, Jaime, Tyson, and who I guessed was Blurry Man. He looked like someone had plucked a Viking out of Norway and put him in a pair of skinny jeans and a tight band t-shirt. His blond beard was immaculately trimmed, his hair was long with tiny braids here and there, some even looked like they had tiny bones threaded in. My brain took a moment to process what I was seeing.

"She really is, isn't she? Smart too." He nodded his head in almost a bow like gesture in my direction. "Forgive me. I know you've met my boys and Jaime but let me introduce myself. I'm Erik Magnus, but you can call me Magnus."

"How about I call your ass trespassing? Get the hell off my property!" I gestured back the way they had come.

"*Your* property? Don't you mean the Immortal Council's?" He folded his arms, which made his biceps look ridiculously large and his shirt strain. "Let's go inside and have a little chat."

I moved so I was in front of Victor and opened my mouth to tell him where Magnus could shove his chat but he spoke softly to me. "Let's hear them out."

I'm sure my expression said everything without the need of words but seriously, what the actual fuck? No one else had emerged from the house. Maybe they'd all gone to sleep. We were outnumbered and at least one of us had a clear enough head to realize it.

"Fine." They all moved toward the door so I pointed at Magnus. "Just you."

He frowned. "We've come a long way. It would be nice to sit and rest a while."

I motioned behind them. "Find a tree and have a seat. It's either just you, or no one." I turned and marched into the house.

As I suspected, the house was silent, indicating the rest had moved to the lower levels. While the sun didn't burn, it may have still drained them. There must be more to it. Something I hadn't figured out yet.

My feet took a right and I found a spot in the parlor where I could still see the driveway, as well as the three rogues who had taken my suggestion and found a spot outside to sit. Victor followed me in and was now sitting to my left.

Magnus took his time checking out the entryway and the room before sitting across from me. The delicate chair strained under his bulk and I realized that must be why Steve always stood when we were in this room. I'd mention that to Dona later.

"You wanted to talk?" I unfolded my arms and gestured in his direction. "Start talking."

He nodded and sat forward, resting his elbows on his knees. "I'm sorry about the poison. We had to know if you were worthy. If your clan wasn't willing to save you, you wouldn't have been worth our time."

I felt Victor tense beside me and it took everything I had not to turn his direction. The man in front of me was sizing me up. If I ever needed to be a leader, it was now. Loathing kept my eyes pinned on Erik Magnus.

"You almost killed one of my reborn with that poison. Not really a great way to start a friendship."

"That poison shouldn't have affected reborn." He looked surprised then figured it out. "Unless they didn't start out that way. Rumor has it that you weren't interested in growing your clan."

"You know what they say about rumors. What do you want?"

He sat back and opened his arms. "You and I want the same thing. To get the Council out of our lives. But looking at this place, I can see why you might not be so keen to walk away. What about your clan? Are they happy with how the Council keeps them under their thumb?" His eyes ticked to Victor. "How about you? I'm sure you'd be happier not waiting for that death sentence to be fulfilled, right?"

I waved my hands to get his attention. "Hey, hi! Remember me, you said you wanted to talk to me. Why don't you leave my people out of it?"

He smiled. "They've got their hooks in you already. You're even starting to act like them. Your *clan* is supposed to be your family. You are not a queen, no matter what the Council tells you."

"My clan *is* my family and we're not interested in joining your little club. Thanks for stopping by."

Magnus pulled his phone from his back pocket, which looked very strange in his hands. Vikings didn't have phones, plus it looked ridiculously small in his huge mitts. He opened an app and set it on the table between us.

"Scroll through. I'm sure some of these would be very interesting to the Council."

I picked up the phone then glanced outside. Tyson was no longer visible. This had gone on long enough, or so I thought until I looked at the phone. It was pictures. Pictures of Victor and me in Utah, some of me sitting with Sam at the bar, Acacia and Eve standing outside in the sun, and the last one was Victor and I standing together just now. That one gave me pause but not because it was so damning, but because of the way I was looking at him. Again, my personal life could wait.

"So?" I feigned.

"The Council is too self-absorbed to figure out why only rogues can be in the sun. You however, figured it out in a matter of days. When they see these, they will think you've joined us whether you have or not. Especially him. They can't wait for him to disappear."

My mouth started moving before my brain. "And why is that?"

Magnus smiled and sat forward, gesturing for the phone. "He doesn't fit with what they have planned for you."

I placed the phone face down in my lap. "No one has that much power over me."

"Arabella, you're late to this game. They hold all the cards. Everything you have, they own and control. Even your people can get taken away. Just ask Seraphine."

This time I did look at Victor because he was there when she was sentenced. His expression was stone. I'd seen that look before. He thought it made him look intimidating and to some I'm sure it did, but it told me he was scared.

Victor finally spoke. "He's right. All of Seraphine's people were given to other clans, including yours, until the Council sees that she is fit enough to have them back."

"You've figured out that first generations are the key to being in the sun. As I'm sure you've deduced that despite what the Council says, you are not the only first generation living immortal." Erik began then shook his head. "First generation is a misnomer. Clearly you come from a long line of vampires, as do I and my sons. Yet we have all the characteristics of someone whose parents both carried the silent mutation making us *look* like first generations. In reality, the gene goes dormant for a few generations until it is needed again."

"You're losing me." I tapped my foot.

"Why are you a living immortal but your sister is not? Because you are the first born. Sam is a living immortal but Tyson is not for the same reason."

"Yeah, I read something like that in the Council books."

"Here's something you didn't read. You really are the first female 'first generation' living immortal. You are a unicorn and they plan on placing you in a butterfly jar until they figure out what you can do."

His words gave me pause. My brain scanned the information from the Council chest plus everything Dona had tried to squish into my head. There was nothing about first generation living immortals. We were an unknown and therefore, a threat.

"How many first generation living immortal men are there?"

"Now you're catching on." Magnus winked and tilted his head to the side. "However, I'm not really inclined to share all our secrets just yet. You need to talk with your clan. We'll be back at midnight to continue this conversation. Keep the phone. Everything has been transferred to the cloud so we have copies. Get some sleep. I promise no harm will come to you or yours before that time."

Something in his tone made me believe him, not that I was sure I could sleep with all this new information. He got up and walked out of the house. Sam, Jaime, and Tyson followed him up the driveway without a backwards glance.

. . . .

MY PHONE CHIRPED AT 10PM making sure I didn't sleep too long. Surprisingly, it had indeed come despite my whirling mind. The resulting nightmares didn't help and I felt groggy. I'd gone with Victor to his rooms because I hadn't wanted to be alone. Now that I was awake and thinking clearly, I realized what a selfish decision that was. We were so far removed from the others that the rogues could have come in and slaughtered everyone while we slept.

I rolled over to face him. "I need you to promise me something."

He gave me a soft kiss. "Anything."

I sat up and pulled my knees to my chest. "If Acacia goes with them, I need you to go too."

"I'm not going to leave you, and neither is she."

"You don't see how much she blames me for what happened to Eve. I need time to fix that and we don't have any. Promise me."

"I promise but you're worrying about nothing. No one is leaving."

I wasn't so sure. My sister and I had always struggled and I may have pushed too hard too fast this time. Deep down, she knew I'd never do anything to hurt Eve but right now she was too upset to think clearly.

Eve's laughter relaxed some of my tension as we entered the kitchen. Rowan and Steve were drinking tea at the table. The delicate cup looked ridiculous in Steve's huge hand. Eve and Acacia were mixing lemonade, or at least attempting to as most of the powder was going everywhere but in the pitcher. Dona sat at the breakfast bar typing on her tablet, a large glass of red wine within reach. I hated to ruin the mood.

Rowan noticed us first. "Today's test was a success! We should celebrate. I think we still have tequila and gin. Oh, never mind, I finished the gin."

"Actually, we..." I started but Dona interrupted without looking up.

"Arabella, do you know why your accounts are frozen?"

I ignored her question because it wasn't the most pressing thing. "After our little walk in the sun, the rogues popped in for a visit while everyone celebrated by taking a nap."

The only sound was the hum of the refrigerator. Everyone stopped what they were doing and turned to look at me. Expressions ranged from fear to anger. Victor put his hand on my back for support.

"And you are just telling us now?" Rowan stood.

"There wasn't any reason to keep you from sleeping. It was more important that everyone rested. They'll be back at midnight to talk."

Rowan started yelling directions at everyone so I went to the coffee maker and started it up. No one was listening to him anyway, too busy processing the bomb I just dropped. After I had a full mug in my hand, I turned around.

"Are you finished?" I asked him. He looked around to see that no one had moved so he nodded. "Good. We learned a bit about who we are dealing with and what they want. Everyone get comfortable, we don't have a lot of time."

I gave the CliffNotes version of the meeting earlier today. There weren't many questions and a lot of silence after, which concerned me. Had I really been so easily indoctrinated by the Council? Was Erik right that I had been blinded by their lies?

As I was refilling my coffee mug for the third time, Dona approached me. "Can I talk to you for a second?"

I glanced at my watch. "You have about two minutes if Erik is punctual and for some reason he seems like that kinda guy."

She opened her mouth to speak as the doorbell rang. A mixture of shock and fear crossed her face a second before she wrapped her arms my middle and whispered, "I'm so sorry."

"Sorry for what?" I called as she bolted from the room.

The front door opened and I could hear Rowan and Erik's voices, neither sounded happy. With a long wistful look at my fresh cup of coffee, I joined them in the entryway. There had been no discussion about who was invited in tonight but it appeared it was just Erik and Sam. Somehow, I doubted the others were too far away. How many was another matter.

"I'd offer you a coffee but you're not staying that long."

Erik gave me that head bob slash bow thing again and it made my skin crawl. Sam just grinned at me like he had in Utah. The reminder of his betrayal made me want to punch that smug look off his face.

Instead, I motioned toward the parlor. "Shall we?"

Dona had moved in a couple sturdier chairs during her mad dash from the kitchen to the parlor. They looked out of place but at least the bigger guys now had somewhere to sit. After a quick glance around the room, I noticed we were missing someone.

"Where's Steve?"

Rowan answered. "He's outside entertaining the rest of the party."

I didn't like the sound of that. Steve was more than capable but how many more were out there? This never felt like a friendly conversation, now it felt like a siege.

"No need to repeat your spiel from this morning. Everyone's up to speed," I said as I sat near Eve and Acacia.

Erik smiled. "I think we got off on the wrong foot."

"Poisoning people and blackmail tend to do that." I held his gaze.

He looked away first, scanning the faces of my clan. "We didn't come here to fight. We're here to give you an option. Unlike the Immortal Council, our goal isn't to make you cogs in a machine. You're immortals, not indentured servants."

"What does that mean?" Acacia asked, sitting forward.

Dammit. I knew this would happen and was powerless to stop it. Well, I could but it would just make their point and make her hate me forever. So, I sat there and tried not to audibly grind my teeth.

Erik smiled warmly at her. "Acacia, you are something special. The Council has unofficially blocked the rebirth of first generations for a very long time since they are usually harder to control. Chatelain slipped the ban into the 'rules' years ago without the Council actually voting on it. While the rest of your clan will need living immortal assistance to walk in the sun, you do not."

"Yep. Already knew that," she said, sitting back and folding her arms across her chest. "But what can you offer me that she, uh I mean, they can't?"

My heart broke a little. She hated me and was looking for any reason to leave. No matter what he said next, she was lost to me. How did she not know how much I loved her? That I was willing to do anything for her? My time to show her was up.

"The Council has so many rules for reborn, it's impossible to really live. While we don't promise absolute lawlessness, we let you have the freedom you'll never have with them." His eyes flicked to mine. "You don't even have to leave your clan. Like I said earlier, we're not here to fight. We want all of you to stand with us."

The way he looked at me now really made my skin crawl. He didn't need any of my people. He only wanted me. His words this morning came rushing back. *You are a unicorn and they plan on placing you in a butterfly jar until they figure out what you can do.* Looks like the Council wasn't the only one with that plan.

"Arabella, you're not like them. You are one of us whether you realize it or not," Sam started but Erik cut him off.

"My son is right, of course. You have already pushed back more in the last six months than anyone has in decades."

"You mean besides the homicidal bitch Seraphine?" I was already tired of his bullshit.

He nodded. "That was a bit different. You actually want change. She just wanted to overthrow the Council."

I did want change but this didn't feel like the way to do it. The boat had already been rocked with Chatelain being forced to step down and the Council now on a lottery appointment system rather than a lifelong seat. We could make it better, but it wasn't clear what Erik was proposing.

I looked around the room and studied my clan. Acacia had shifted her body away from me, Rowan looked ready to explode, Eve fidgeted under the tension, and Dona wouldn't look at me or our visitors. When she finally did make eye contact with me, she looked terrified. Some would leave; the rest would suffer if I made the wrong decision. They were my family and depended on me.

"Okay. You've talked. We've listened." I rose from my chair. "We'll think about what you said and let you know."

Erik stood and moved so he was inches from me. Both Victor and Rowan tensed but stayed where they were. Eve clutched Acacia's arm and looked away. Living immortal or not, a sharp knee to the groin would drop this mother fucker if he tried anything.

"I hadn't planned on leaving without an answer."

"Plans change." I held my ground despite the fact he towered over me.

He stepped back and winked at me as if nothing had happened. My brain short circuited for a second as he moved to stand behind his chair. Massive hands gripped the back and the chair groaned under his weight. I'd expected a different reaction to my blatant defiance and wasn't sure how to process what was happening.

"War on the Immortal Council begins this day. Pick a side. We won't ask again."

His eyes were roaming my clan but landed on mine last. Suddenly, he looked every bit the savage he was. He wanted a battle. He lived for it.

Acacia stood and I sucked in a breath. She looked at me for a moment as if she was searching for any reason to stay. I had nothing to give and her expression hardened. She pulled Eve up with her.

"No, Acacia," Eve whined and tried to pull her back down. "We can't leave. Arabella needs us."

Acacia dropped her hand like it was fire. "Fine. Stay and be her slave. I'm done."

Erik turned to Dona. "Daughter, are you coming?"

My mouth literally dropped open. I looked from Erik to Sam then to Dona. How had I not seen it before? The shape of her face and nose. Her eyes were blue though. She stood and gave me a sad smile. Slowly, she took off her giant glasses then removed her colored contacts. Gold irises looked back at me. I swear she looked like she was trembling in fear.

"Anyone else?" Erik turned his gaze back to me.

I'd never seriously contemplated murder. I'd even back peddled when it came to Seraphine who clearly wanted me dead. But now, I wished I could blow this asshole away. My hands clenched at my sides and I hoped the depth of my hatred showed in my expression.

To my left Victor stood and for a moment, I forgot about the promise he'd made me. My posture shift must have been convincing because Erik chuckled. So much for me not being able to lie.

Victor walked over and pulled me close, one hand against my waist, the other tangled in my hair. His lips brushed against my cheek and his voice was so low I was sure no one could hear but me. "I'll keep her safe."

When he released me and stepped back, I kept the charade going with an actual tear because losing them was tearing me apart. "You don't have to do this. There must be another way."

"The Council wants me dead for loving you. Maybe this is how I get my chance."

Erik frowned at Victor's words and my resolve started to slip. Clearly, Victor wasn't part of his plan for me either. I knew if he walked out that door, I would never see him again. What could I do?

"What is it that you want from the Council?" I turned back to face Erik. "If I tell you now that I will join your little crusade, what is the goal?"

"*Is* that what you're saying?" I hesitated and he nodded. "I didn't think so. You don't like bullies so forcing your hand won't help my cause. Our goal is freedom. We want it and so do you. Think about what I said for a few days. You can contact me with the only number programmed in that phone I gave you this morning."

Without another word, he turned and walked out of my house. Acacia, Victor, and Dona followed while Sam brought up the rear. He gave a salute to Rowan who was trembling but with rage, not fear. Eve put her face in her hands and started to sob.

Chapter Eighteen

"How could you just let them leave?" Eve asked once the headlights disappeared down the driveway.

I walked out of the room without answering. My feet carried me outside where I paced. Erik's plan to destroy the Immortal Council wasn't actually a terrible idea but somehow, I felt like he was leaving something out. He said he was giving us a choice but he never specified the alternative.

"Steve! We need you back inside. Steve?"

There was no answer. He wouldn't have left my clan. It was the first thing he'd ever chosen for himself. He had more freedom here with us than ever before. I checked the front of the house then the garage side. By the time I got to the fairy lights, I was running and screaming his name.

When I found him, he was lying on his side in a pool of light and my feet stilled. Rowan came up behind me then cursed. He moved to Steve and gently turned him on his back. He was covered in bruises and shallow cuts. Eve joined me but when she tried to lurch forward, I pulled her against me.

"No. They can't take everyone," she cried.

Rowan sat back on his heels. "He's not dead permanently. It looks like someone beat him senseless then broke his neck. He'll need blood and a few days, but he'll be okay."

Eve slumped in my arms and I held her as she cried with relief. I was too angry to join her. Instead, I led her back into the house and put my now cold cup of coffee in front of her.

"Stay here. We'll be right back."

Rowan and I carried Steve to his room and placed him on the bed. He was very solid and heavy, even for our immortal strength. I'd only ever peeked in from the hallway before. Even though we all lived together, I tried to give everyone space for privacy, even though the favor wasn't necessarily returned.

His room was the definition of utilitarian. There was a neatly made bed, nightstand holding a Western paperback, small dresser, and a floor lamp in the corner. No other personal touches other than a painting of a sunlit forest. When I neared the art, I noticed Acacia's signature at the bottom.

That's what did me in. Tears blurred my vision. There were no good options. My clan was reduced to myself, an angry Brit, and a newborn. Eve was barely holding it together so I'm not sure if she actually counted yet. If I reached out to the Council they would put Victor and Acacia on the rogue list. Dona too but I didn't know how I felt about her betrayal yet.

I was so tired of being used. Rowan put his arms around me and let me cry it out but didn't placate me by saying everything would be okay. My refusal to join Erik was the same as siding with the Council. I'd damned the remainder of my clan and most likely myself in the process. When I was done with my most recent pity party, I wiped my eyes and stepped back.

"What do we do now?" I asked.

"We need to contact the Council, clearly." Rowan threw his hands up dramatically.

I shook my head. "They'll punish Acacia and Victor. There has to be another option. Let's go see what else Dona's been hiding."

I'd never been in her room either and she'd kept the door shut. I blinked several times when I flipped on the light. Everything was shades of purple and white. While Steve's room was all purpose, Dona's was all frill. I mean who uses doilies anymore? Old timey kitten prints hung on the wall in ornate gold frames.

"If this doesn't look like a serial killer's room, I don't know what does," Rowan said as he joined me in the space.

"Look in the closet. I've got the dresser," I said as I opened the top drawer.

Socks and stockings were rolled neatly and placed in a drawer organizer, moving in the colors of the rainbow from left to right. The next drawer appeared to be tights and leggings, all meticulously folded. Underwear and pajamas rounded out the dresser. Everything was neat and orderly to the point of mental illness. When I turned to the closet, it looked the same. Clothes were organized by kind then color. Shoes were in neat rows on a shoe rack on the back of the door. Hat boxes lined the top shelves, which was interesting because I'd never seen her wear a hat except for the sun hat yesterday.

"Grab the boxes," I said to Rowan.

He handed me the first one. Inside was a red felt hat, very 1920's and nothing else. We went through five more before we found something interesting. This box held photos and they were not neatly stacked or organized in any way. The first set were grainy black and white images of children, two boys and two girls. They were laughing while playing in a river. The next set showed a picture of a teenage Dona wearing a flapper style dress. Another girl who looked strikingly similar stood behind her and slightly out of focus, both their hair was done up in tiny ringlets. Dona was posing in a dramatic fashion. The next in the series was a close up of her laughing with her hand up as if to stop the photographer.

The stack on the bottom showed a very different tone. Dona looked as she does now. The smile and happiness were missing from her eyes, even in pictures when she was actually smiling. The round glasses appeared and never left. The final picture was of Dona and Erik. He stood beside her with his arm around her shoulders. She looked tiny and frightened.

"She's being forced to do this. That's why she apologized to me tonight. She was terrified and didn't want to leave." I handed the photo to Rowan. "We have to get them back, all of them."

"How?" Rowan put the lid back on the box.

"We're going to play their game."

• • • •

EVE WAS STILL SITTING in the kitchen, staring at the empty coffee mug when we returned. I guess I had told her to stay but it wasn't a demand. While she seemed to be recovering from her transition, her brain wasn't firing on all cylinders yet. I understood because I knew what it felt like when you thought you'd lost everything.

"I don't want to be alone. Can I sleep with you?" she asked as I led her back to Acacia's room as hers was still a disaster area.

"Sure, but I'm not going to sleep yet." She opened her mouth to protest but I continued, "You need to rest and I need to make a phone call. I'll be back soon."

She sank onto the bed and smashed her face into the pillows. I heard sobbing but I couldn't stay. The room reminded me of what I was losing so I hurried to the office.

"Are you sure about this?" Rowan asked me for the fifth time.

I pressed call on my cell followed by the speaker button. The ringtone sounded odd but apparently that's what overseas calls did. Rowan stood on the other side of the desk, looking less than convinced. My hand reached to end the call when a deep voice answered.

"Hello?"

I sank into the chair with relief. Please let this be the right decision. "Joseph. It's Arabella. Are you free to talk?"

There was a brief pause. "Of course, what can I do for you?"

Rowan and I looked at each other before he quickly answered for me. "It's about our mutual friend."

Another longer pause followed by muffled voices. Rowan reached over to hang up the phone but I pulled it closer to me. We needed help but the Council was not it.

"My apologies for the delay. I am free to speak with you now," Joseph said when he returned to the line.

My foot tapped as I organized my words. "How much do you know about the rogue problem?"

"Quite a bit. What do you want to know?"

"Everything, but we don't have time. They recruited half my clan, our friend included." Even though he said he was free to talk, I was hesitant to use names.

"What can I do to help?" His request seemed genuine and Rowan seemed to relax.

"You know as well as I do that the Immortal Council is broken. Erik Magnus aims to destroy it entirely no matter who gets in his way."

"And you're sure he's wrong?"

Rowan and I stared at each other in disbelief. The hairs on my arms rose as a feeling of dread swept over me. How deep did this go? Had I really chosen the wrong side?

I changed the course of the conversation. "You told Rowan there was a failed attempt on Chatelain's life."

"That is true. He has been moved for his safety. You may wish to do the same."

"Are you telling us this because you know something?" Rowan's voice made me jump.

"Rowan, you and I both know that no harm will come to Arabella. However, I cannot say the same for her clan."

A notification of another call started flashing on the screen. I moved to swipe to ignore it but the ID read Dona.

"I'm sorry but I have to go. Can I call you back?"

"Any time. I'm always here for a friend."

I quickly disconnected and answered the other call. "Dona? Are you still there?"

Her voice was a rushed whisper and I heard another conversation in the background. "I left my tablet under the hutch in the parlor. I never meant to hurt you or the clan. I'm so sorry."

The call went dead and both Rowan and I rushed to the front of the house. I was grateful that his sun immunity was holding because he didn't stop until we were in the parlor, which was currently filled with sunshine.

I dropped to my knees and started looking under everything. What exactly was a hutch? There was a tall cabinet with glass doors in the corner, something thin and black was under it. I scrambled over and turned on the tablet. Dozens of apps and icons appeared. How was this supposed to be helpful?

"There." Rowan pointed at a folder with my name on it.

I opened it and it too was full of icons. Luckily, they were all well labeled. Had she really called so I had my calendar? The folder had account information, contact lists, grocery inventory, meeting notes, and everything else related to keeping the house. It looked like she was doing her and Rowan's jobs. None of it looked useful, until I found a folder without a label.

I clicked on it and discovered another untitled document. There was no formatting and the words ran together as if she was trying to write it without looking at the screen and in a hurry. I thought back to our meeting with Erik and how she wouldn't make eye contact with anyone. She was writing this and hoped no one noticed.

Every word he speaks is lies. He told me he was the only one who could protect me from the sun. That's why I was so scared. He's doing this because he wants to rule, not give freedom. I joined Seraphine's clan as a spy and a way to send funds to my father because I believed he could free us. I joined your clan for the same reason but then we became friends. By then it was too late to stop and I didn't want you to send me away. He doesn't want a partner for this war. He doesn't need more soldiers. He wants a wife. He thinks he can breed first generation living immortals. Send the money so he doesn't know I failed. He killed my sister for less. Please.

I sat back and handed the tablet to Rowan. He had been reading over my shoulder but took time to read it again.

"I'm confused," Rowan said.

I gave him an exasperated look. "You and me both. I had no idea Dona was doing your job too."

He frowned at me. "Not the takeaway I believe Dona was going for but yes, some of it. She says Erik wants to breed living immortals. Female living immortals can't have children after their death. They've tried for generations."

"Unicorn, remember?" I pointed at my eyes. "Not that I think he's right. I've been pregnant twice and neither turned out well."

Rowan froze then turned to face me. "Could you repeat that last part?"

"It's not something I'm proud of but I got knocked up after a one-night stand in college and had a miscarriage before I even realized I was pregnant. That ninety-eight percent effective notice on the condom wrapper was no joke. You know what happened the second time."

Rowan grabbed my face and planted a big kiss on my lips then started to laugh. His reaction made no sense. It wasn't funny and I hadn't told anyone except my college roommate who had to drive me home from the hospital. I'd even used a fake name and cash at the hospital, afraid my parents would somehow find out.

"Rowan, you've gone completely mad. Could you keep it together until after we get the rest of the clan back?"

He continued to laugh. "I apologize for every negative thing I've ever said about you. Apparently, you can keep secrets so well not even the Immortal Council can figure them out."

Chapter Nineteen

I'd reached out to Erik last night about a meeting, just the two of us. If he wanted my trust, he'd have to earn it since his attempts thus far had been piss poor. Rowan had reluctantly stayed at the house with Eve. She was starting to slip back into mania so I needed to make sure to bring her some blood.

The overhead music at my favorite coffee shop was decent today. Usually, I got my cup to go because the owner was into some really random shit. The last time it had been Tibetan throat singing. It wasn't bad at first but it got old really fast.

Rich coffee aroma mingled with the sweetness of pastries. My eyes roamed over the few other occupants, most hunched over their laptops or staring at their phones. The giant globe sculpture made of wine bottles made me think of Victor. The continents had been shaped out of red wine bottles while the oceans were either white or rosé. He was one of the reasons I was here. I needed my family back. Once that happened, we'd all share several bottles of Victor's favorite red wine.

Erik sauntered in and stopped to order a drink. I sipped mine and picked at my almond pastry while I waited. We were about to see if I was as capable of lying as I was keeping secrets, as Rowan so delicately put it.

Once he had his coffee in hand, he graced me with a smile that I'm sure made other women swoon. The barista was currently pouring cream onto the counter so he'd apparently frozen her brain when he'd picked up his drink.

He sat across from me at the tiny table. "I've been looking forward to your call."

I nodded and took another bite of my pastry. It was a stall tactic. I really disliked the man in front of me but I needed to pretend otherwise. The goal was resting bitch face and from the slip in his smile, I think I nailed it.

I wiped my hands on a napkin. "I've thought about what you said. While I'm not one hundred percent for your plan, I'm not completely against it either. You've been less than kind to my clan so I'm going to need some reassurances if we're going to work together."

He took a sip of his coffee and I enjoyed how he recoiled at the temperature. I was pretty sure they used lava as their coffee base. You needed a good ten to fifteen minutes before you could savor the first sip safely. I considered it a tiny victory and did my best to hide my amused grin.

"We're on the same team here, Arabella."

"Are we though? You've left me without options. My clan has been reduced to two and you have enough evidence to convince the Council that I'm all in with your little war party whether I am or not."

Erik looked down at his hands folded neatly on the table. "There will be consequences for hurting your clan member. That was not part of the plan. I sincerely apologize. Jaime tends to get carried away when challenged."

While his words felt hollow, I forced myself to relax so he thought I believed him. His posture improved so it must have worked. I took another sip of coffee as if this was an everyday coffee date with an old friend.

"The Immortal Council has been forcing me into their nice little box from the start but I keep poking holes in it. If I'm going to join you, I need to know everything. No more secrets."

He sat back and regarded me for a moment before he spoke. "There are currently five first generation living immortals. Three, including myself and Sam, are working to dismantle the Council."

"And the other two?"

"I'm looking at one. The other is content to stay out of the Council's line of sight and I've agreed to let that happen."

I looked down as if upset, which wasn't far from the truth. "How are Acacia and Victor?"

He reached over and put his hand over mine, it basically disappeared. "Adjusting. Your sister has some real anger issues."

I longed to pull my hand back but I kept it still and looked up. "What about Dona?"

This time he sat back and folded his arms. "Busy, but that's what she does best."

"When can I see them?"

"We can go see Acacia and Dona right now if you'd like. Victor, however, is on his way back to the Council."

Panic made me fumble out of character. "What? Why?"

"We needed a bargaining tool to gain an audience with them."

"Then use me. You said they think I'm something special. They'll listen if they really believe that."

Erik sat forward and captured my hand again with a wink. "I knew you were smart."

The computer zombies had surrounded our little table and my wrist was in Eric's death grip. I was an idiot and walked right into his trap. So much for letting me decide.

Computer Zombie One to my left picked up my purse, including my phone, and headed toward the front door. Eric gave my wrist a gentle twist and I grimaced. He could break it with the tiniest twitch.

"Shall we?" he asked with a grin.

"This was never about a partnership, was it?"

He brought us both to our feet. "Perhaps if time was on our side but alas, it never is. I'm sure you'll soon see everything is how it should be."

Erik and his goons walked us out of the coffee shop to a set of SUVs. He opened the door for me then let go of my arm. I squeezed my hand into a fist a few times to get the blood flowing again. When he slid in beside me, I turned to look at him in time to register a fist headed in my direction.

I WOKE UP SOME TIME later lying face down on a couch in what appeared to be an office based on the large wooden desk and bookshelves dominating the space. My skull felt like it was ready to split open and the Sahara had moved into my mouth. There were no windows in the room so I had no sense of the time or even where I was. My purse sat on the table beside me and I quickly opened it. Everything was there except the phone.

"Fuck." I tossed it away then put my head in my hands.

Erik didn't just look strong; he was strong. From the nausea and slightly out of focus vision, I was pretty sure I had a concussion. Yay for my inability to heal. Blinking back blurriness, I noticed a bottle of water across the room.

I hurried over and uncapped the lid. Just before it touched my lips, I remembered they had already poisoned me once but decided it was worth the risk. If they had wanted me dead, I would have never woken up after that punch.

After a few minutes of snooping, I decided to try the only door in the room. Much to my surprise it was unlocked. I poked my head outside and understood why. Jamie stood about ten feet down the hall.

"Arabella! How's it going, girl?"

"You can drop the act. We're not friends," I answered and tried to shoulder past her.

"I'm gonna need you to stay in that room until Erik's ready to see you." She put her hand on my arm. "I don't want to hurt you but I will if you make me."

"Ready or not, here I come." I slapped her hand away and took another step.

She spun around and landed a kick to my back that took my breath away. When I stood and faced her, she was in full fighter's stance, bouncing on the balls of her feet. Despite her words, she was looking for a fight.

"You really want to do this?" I asked.

She made a come-hither motion with her forward hand. I dropped and swept my leg under hers but she anticipated and jumped. Her elbow connected with my shoulder as she came down. My reaction time was slow due to the concussion but I had more at stake than she did. Plus, I had no reason to fight fair.

As I righted myself, she caught me with a quick jab to the chin then she danced back out of my reach. I spit blood at her and lunged, catching her around the waist. The wood floor was slick, plus I had a good fifty pounds on her. We fell into a heap and both struggled for the better position. She pounded my kidneys and I almost lost my grip. It was dirty but I bit down as hard as I could on her arm that I'd pinned between us. Reborn blood filled my mouth and the dizziness was instantly better.

I shifted my hips and lifted until we were standing. She was still wrapped around my torso from behind and I fell like a stone, landing on top. Her back hit the ground with a sickening crunch and her grip faltered long enough for me to adjust and start smashing her face with my fists. Her arms moved to block but it was halfhearted. I'd rung her bell pretty hard.

Slow clapping made me pause. "As entertaining as this is, we have more important matters to attend to."

I sat back on my heels and looked at Erik and Sam. I felt more than saw Jaime move but Sam rushed in to intercept her. He whispered clipped words that seemed to drain her need to fight. Erik looked at her with dead eyes, as if he had no more use for her. There was no doubt she wasn't supposed to hurt me.

"Are you coming?" he asked, turning away from the group.

I followed him down a long hallway and up a flight of stairs. We were clearly in a Council safe house or an equivalent. I could hear people all around but every door we passed was closed. We finally landed in what appeared to be a living room on the main level. I looked out the windows to see a stream and a wall of trees at twilight. We could have been at my next-door neighbor's house or anywhere in this half of the state.

"Can I get you anything?" he asked after pouring himself something from an amber decanter. When I shook my head, he continued, "I apologize for my barbaric methods but we really do need you on this team and you were taking far too long to make a decision."

"You could've just asked." I winced as I sat, kidneys screaming. "On second thought, can I have some of whatever you're having?"

He handed me a glass and I tossed it back. It tasted like someone crapped in a bottle of paint thinner. The cough was an involuntary means to expel the disgusting drink but it made my back hurt even more. Erik laughed and poured me something from a clear bottle.

I carefully sipped the clear liquid and welcomed the familiar flavor of vanilla vodka. Whatever the other bottle held was not fit for human, or vampire, consumption. My stomach rolled as he casually sipped it.

"Now that we're settled, let's get down to business."

I couldn't help but hum the rest of the cheesy song from the cartoon movie whose name escaped me at that moment. From his confused expression, it was not one he recognized. My concussion clearly hadn't fully healed yet—or I'd finally lost my marbles.

"What can this hostage do for you, O' Majestic One?" I asked, finishing my drink.

He frowned. "The Immortal Council needs to be disbanded. I have over half of the living immortals ready to stand with us."

I ignored the 'us' comment and poured myself another glass of vodka. "So, what do you need me and my clan for?"

"Arabella," he said from immediately behind me, making me tense. For someone so big, he was awfully stealthy. "Once the Council falls, the rest of the living immortals will look for someone to lead."

He ran his fingers down my arm and I recoiled, having a bad feeling as to where this was going. "You want me to vouch for you? I'm a nobody. Most of the other living immortals don't even know I exist yet."

He'd boxed me in against the wet bar and I suddenly felt very small. "I want you to sit beside me at the head of the table."

I attempted to swing under his arm to put some space between us but he blocked my escape. "I'm not really management material. Just ask what's left of my clan."

He flattened the palm of his hand on my stomach, splaying his huge fingers and pressing slightly, and I wanted to throw up. "We don't need the rest of them. We can create our own."

I gently moved his hand away. "I'm going to take a hard pass on that one. If you haven't noticed, female living immortals can't have kids once their mortal life ends. You're about two years too late. Besides, I've already met the one guy who I'm genetically compatible with and he's moved on to someone else."

Erik threw his head back and started to laugh. Nothing I just said was funny. Nothing he said was funny. I crossed my arms and waited for him to finish. This man was a complete nutcase.

"That old wives' tale is still going around? Arabella, two of my three children came from different women, none of them were mere humans."

I tried to counter his jab at my ignorance with one of my own. "You mean four, don't you?"

His expression darkened and he stepped back. "What you are failing to grasp is this will happen whether you agree to it or not. We are the chosen rulers. You will come to accept that."

"And we're back to threatening. Why don't you ask Victor about how well that works for me?" As soon as the words left my mouth, I mentally slapped myself. Why couldn't I keep my mouth closed?

Erik smiled at me. "Your loyalty will be your undoing."

He pounded on the wall above my head and the door opened. Tyson appeared and waited for instruction. He looked as emotionless

153

as he had the last two times I'd seen him. I wondered how he felt about being used like Dona.

"Our guest would like to visit her sister." He turned back to me. "We don't have to be enemies, Arabella. That choice *is* entirely up to you."

Chapter Twenty

Tyson and I walked in silence as I tried to make sense of the house layout. We left in a different direction than Erik had taken me but somehow, we still ended up going back down to the lower levels. I doubted the maze was a coincidence.

"How do you feel about Daddy's world domination plans?" I asked as we descended another set of stairs.

"I don't care either way."

Tyson's voice was not at all what I expected. It was higher in pitch and I felt like I almost caught a speech impediment. If he truly was indifferent, I needed to keep him talking. Clearly, I wasn't getting out of here on my own.

"Is that because he treats you and Dona like second class citizens? You know, because you aren't living immortals like Sam?"

He rounded on me and I knew I'd struck a nerve. "Being a living immortal doesn't automatically put you in his favor or make you exempt from his punishment."

I continued walking and pondered his words then took a leap of faith. "Is that what happened to your other sister?"

This time his hand roughly grabbed my upper arm and he turned me back to face him. "He'll throw you away too when he no longer needs you. Useless things are beneath him. Remember that."

"Thanks for the tip. Can I see my sister now?" I shrugged as if he hadn't given me exactly what I wanted.

This man clearly hated his father but, like Dona, was willing to suffer his wrath to continue to be useful and alive. While Erik made the Immortal Council out to be slave owners, he obviously ran his reborn clan with fear and tyranny.

"Second door on your left." He dropped my arm and stood in the hallway, preventing me from heading back the way we'd come.

I knocked lightly on the door then pushed it open. Acacia was sitting on a bed with a sketch book in her lap. The pencil hovered above the page when she looked up. At first, her expression was that of shock then quickly rearranged to her normal annoyed expression. She was wearing the same clothes she had left in but otherwise looked no worse for wear.

"Why are you here?" she asked, looking back at her sketch.

I sat on the chair next to the bed. "Originally, the plan was to spring you, Victor, and Dona from the giant crazy man but now it appears I'm just as stuck as you are."

She nodded and continued to slowly move her pencil over the page. "How's Eve?"

"Devastated that you left. Her transition is not going as smoothly as yours. She kinda needs you right now."

"She changed because of me. I didn't ask her to but I know that's why she rushed into it." Her eyes dropped to the paper. "If she hadn't wanted to be reborn, she wouldn't have been poisoned. It was easier to blame you than myself. I should have never left but I was so mad at everyone. Thanks for trying to save me."

I joined her on the bed and put my arm around her shoulder. She leaned into me and I looked down at her drawing. It wasn't cohesive. There were detailed flowers in one corner then perfect animals that slowly deteriorated into stick figures moving in a jagged line from the middle to the other edge. The sun was above all but looked like it had been drawn by a kindergartener and the circle looped over and over in angry strokes.

"Acacia, when was the last time you had blood?"

She shook her head. "I don't remember. I've been so worried about Eve, I guess I forgot and they haven't let me out of this room since we got here."

"Where's Victor and Dona? Have you seen them?"

She shook her head again. Victor had blood more recently and was out of the transition stage so he could go a little longer but not much. Regardless, the rogues appeared to be neglecting their newest recruits. If my guess was right, they'd unleash them when the blood rage was at a peak. This was just another way to force my hand with the Council.

"Do you still have your phone?" I asked.

She handed it to me but it was dead. Dona's comment about Erik's lies made me wonder if Victor was still here somewhere too. There was no way I could go searching but I knew someone who could. I needed to find Dona and get us the hell out of here.

I gave my sister one more squeeze. "I need to talk to Dona. Stay here and if anyone tries to move you, scream like there's no tomorrow. I'll come running."

She went back to coloring in the sun and I knew her focus was failing. If I didn't get us out of here soon, she wouldn't be safe to move. What I wouldn't give for a phone charger!

I poked my head out the door to see Tyson standing in the exact same spot. At least it didn't appear he was eavesdropping. His posture tensed at my quick reappearance.

"Take me to Dona," I said.

"No."

"I didn't realize I'd asked a question. Erik told me I could see her and Acacia once I arrived. Should we go back and ask Daddy for permission? He seems like a guy who loves to repeat himself."

Tyson let out an annoyed breath and gestured for me to go ahead of him back the way we'd come. He wouldn't speak to me again even though I tried to engage twice. We stopped at a set of double doors and he indicated for me to open them.

I pushed them inward and saw Dona in what appeared to be a small library. Her face was too close to a computer screen and she pushed her glasses up as if to see better. There was no need for the colored contacts here. The gold of her irises still looked so foreign.

She didn't look up until the doors bumped closed. Her expression froze and she blinked a few times as if she wasn't sure if I was really here. Slowly, she got to her feet and stood next to the desk, her expression wary.

I met her in the middle of the room and spoke softly. "I got your message."

"And?" her voice was cautious.

"And we need to get the hell out of here."

Her shoulders dropped and the quick look of relief was replaced by defeat. "We can't. He won't let us."

"Not with that attitude." I moved her to the back of the room in case Tyson decided this was a conversation worth listening in on.

"Leaving won't help. He'll just find us—find me—again," Dona explained.

My shoulders sagged at her words. She was right. Running away wasn't going to solve this problem. My eyes scanned the room looking for answers and found nothing.

"Where are we anyway?" I asked.

"Rental property just west of town," she answered then added, "It's under your name. Sorry."

"Whatever. It's not like it's actually my money. We have bigger problems." I lowered my voice again. "Is Victor still here?"

"Of course, Erik's not going to let him out of his sight. You are too important to his plan. Victor and Acacia are his leverage."

"Where do you stand on all this? Honestly." I gestured toward a set of chairs.

We sat and she took off her glasses. "Once upon a time, I actually had dreams and goals. Now, I just do what other people tell me. I'm tired of belonging to someone."

"So, you think Erik's right?"

"He used to be but as he gained power and influence, he's become as bad or worse as the Council. He can't see it over his ego and just wants to trade one group of tyrants for a single ruler because he thinks he can do so much better. Before I joined your clan, I would have said yes without hesitation. You were so different and gave us as much freedom as you could. That is what we should be working toward."

"Who else here agrees with you?"

Dona's eyes flicked toward the door. "Tyson, maybe a few others. I told you that Erik murdered my sister but that wasn't entirely true. Moriah was Tyson's older sister and my half-sister. She was a first generation living immortal and once Erik's mind was so twisted with world domination, he raped her to create a superior race. She did get pregnant but she killed herself and the baby."

My brain had trouble comprehending this. First, the fact that he raped his own daughter was beyond repulsive and spoke to how bat shit crazy he was. Second, he had proof that female living immortals could have children after their mortal life ended. That was something I needed to seriously think about. Once we survived this mess, that is. One thing was absolutely clear, I was not going to be alone with that man again.

"Can I borrow your phone?" She hesitated so I pressed on. "I'm not leaving any of you but I need to protect the rest of my clan."

She went back to the desk and retrieved it from the drawer. I scanned the contacts for Rowan but didn't find him.

"He's under Useless Brit."

"Clever." I pressed the contact and listened as it rang. It went to voicemail and I wanted to scream. "Rowan, I've been held up. Take Joseph's advice and take Eve on holiday. I'll be in touch."

He was going to be pissed but hopefully he would listen. I needed to know they were out of harm's way. They had his hearse so they could travel at night and be protected in the trunk coffins during the day. Rowan would make sure Eve was safe and had what she needed. He wasn't really useless; he just needed the right motivation.

Dona pulled me from my thoughts when she asked, "How are we going to kill my father?"

I halted the conversation at this point. Murder was not really my go-to plan, even if it seemed to be the norm for other immortals. You'd think permanent death would be scarier to these people but it seemed to be the catch-all solution.

Tyson collected me a short while later. Dona and I had a tentative plan but it required getting to the Council first. That part I wasn't really uncomfortable with. We didn't have the numbers if anything went wrong. She promised to get word to Victor.

Tyson once again wouldn't speak to me as we walked through the house. This time we stopped by the kitchen. He opened the fridge and handed me a water bottle and a paper bag, which I assumed had food in it. Finally, he stopped in front of Acacia's room.

"I thought you would like to stay with your sister."

I searched his expression and words for something hidden. His gesture seemed genuine and maybe he understood how much I cared about her. I opened my mouth to say something about Moriah but closed it. Dona said she'd speak to him. I was a stranger. My words would mean nothing.

"Thanks," I said, then stepped into Acacia's room.

The sun was about to rise, so she had already crashed on her bed. The notepad had fallen into a heap on the floor. I picked it up and flipped through the pages. The first few were sketches of our house from unique angles. There was one of Eve laughing. The last was the disjointed image I'd seen earlier. The sun was now a black hole that ripped through the next page.

I took a seat in the chair and opened the bag. There was a turkey sandwich, an apple, and a plastic bag. I put the first two items aside and pulled out the bag. My brain took a second to understand what I was seeing. I sent Tyson a silent thank you. I held another blood bag in my hand. Looked like I had another ally after all.

• • • •

A HAND ON MY SHOULDER woke me up from a dead sleep. I shouldn't have crashed that hard but once I'd snuggled up against my sister, I'd let my guard down. I hadn't really slept well in days so maybe it was inevitable.

Tyson stood next to the bed and in a low voice whispered, "You need to come with me."

I rubbed the sleep from my eyes and followed him down the hall, yawning the whole way. After a quick glance at my watch, I realized I'd slept almost thirteen hours. Considering how out of it I was, I wondered if my sandwich had been drugged, making me reconsider Tyson's loyalty. My stretch reminded me of the beating I'd taken yesterday. Since Acacia was already struggling, there was no way I was going to take her blood to heal. I'd need to come up with something else.

This time, he took me outside and around the side of the house near a small stream. The sun was dropping below the tree line and the sparse clouds looked like pink cotton candy. There were two large wooden structures on round bases. Rough targets had been painted on them. A light from the side of the house illuminated the entire area like a weird outdoor stage.

Erik stood shirtless near a huge tree stump that held four axes. Thick, black tattoos covered his chest and upper arms. I wondered how that worked since all my scars were long gone and I assumed the same healing would erase tattoos as well. His hair was pulled back into a hasty looking ponytail, making him look very much like Sam.

"Did you sleep well?" Erik asked. When I nodded, he continued, "I was extremely pleased when ax throwing came back into fashion. Have you ever tried?"

The image of an ax buried in his forehead flashed in my mind but he was much closer to the weapons than I was so I answered genuinely. "No."

"Come. I'll give you a quick lesson."

"Any chance I could have some coffee first?" I asked with another yawn.

He smiled again. "This will wake you up better than any drink."

Somehow, I knew this was more than a recreational time killer. Whatever this was supposed to be, it wouldn't be good but at least I wasn't alone with him. With another yawn, I joined Erik at the stump. He rocked one of the axes free and took a moment to line up with the target. His weight shifted and the ax whizzed through the air and buried itself just to the left of dead center.

"Give it a try." He nodded toward the other axes.

I turned back to look at Tyson. Once again, he was an emotionless guard, watching without interest. Erik had made removing the ax look easy. I ended up having to put my leg on the stump to get enough leverage to get it out. Maybe this was just another way for him to show how powerful he was. Gross.

Facing the target, I thought about how Dona tried to teach Steve darts. It wasn't about how hard you threw, it was about focus and technique. I tried to model Erik's motions but my ax bounced off the edge and onto the grass. The fact that my back was killing me didn't help.

Erik came around the stump as he pulled another ax free like it was nothing. He adjusted my body angle slightly and put the weapon in my hand, adjusting the grip. It would have been so easy to turn and chop into his throat but he'd be expecting that reaction and would block me. Instead, I let out a slow breath and put a little more strength behind this throw. The ax sailed in a straight line and stuck in the board this time. It wasn't anywhere near where I intended but it stuck.

He yanked the last ax from the stump and held it to me, handle first. "Nice improvement."

I nodded and attempted another throw. This landed closer to the quadrant where I'd aimed. It helped imagining Erik's face on the target.

He jogged over and retrieved the four axes. His back was also covered in intricate tattoos and lots of muscles. Overpowering him was not going to be an option.

We'd both thrown at least a dozen more times when I heard voices. My shoulder was starting to ache but I played along until I could figure out what the purpose of this game actually was. Erik was currently retrieving the axes from the targets when I turned toward the sound. A man I didn't recognize was half dragging a smaller figure with bound hands and a bag over their head. My heart stopped for a second when I thought it might be Acacia by the size but the muffled voice quickly dispelled that concern.

The man walked past Tyson and myself, making a bee-line toward the targets. Erik had flipped the structures on their bases so while they still had targets, they also had shackles in the four corners. My breath caught in my throat when I realized what I was looking at.

The unknown man stopped by the target nearest Erik and pulled the bag off his captive's head. Dark hair spilled out, as did profanities. Jaime was shouting in another language but there was no doubt her words were not friendly.

Erik backhanded her and she went silent for a moment. He used the shock to pull her hands over her head and attach the first ring. The other man released her bindings and attached the other hand. He got a nasty kick when he reached for her leg but was able to restrain both of them as well. Her small body was suspended by her arms and she glared daggers at me as if this was my idea.

I'd been frozen in place, unable to comprehend what I was seeing and what I feared was about to happen. Blood pounded in my ears and I missed the additional voices joining us. Another captive was led to my target and I had to fight to control my breathing. This time the bound person didn't fight and the hood wasn't immediately removed. It didn't matter; I knew who it was.

"What the fuck are you doing?" I rounded on Erik as he joined me by the stump.

"Jaime has outlived her usefulness. I assumed you'd want to participate in her punishment since she wronged you directly."

He offered me an ax but I pushed the handle away. "You assumed wrong."

He shrugged and let the first ax fly. It caught the bottom of her upper arm, splitting it to the bone. She screamed and thrashed in an attempt to get away. Blood poured down the wall onto the grass.

"I get it. She didn't listen to you." I grabbed his arm when he lifted the next ax. "I'm sure she's learned her lesson."

Erik shrugged me off and gave me a dark look. "You think the best of people. Admirable trait but also foolish. Jaime is untrustworthy. I have no use for liars."

The second ax tumbled through the air and caught her calf. This time it stuck in the bone. There was one sharp cry then sobbing. Her eyes kept searching behind us as if for rescue, lips whispering Sam's name. I was trying to save her but my words seemed useless. Once again, an ax handle was jabbed my way.

When I refused, he opened my hand and roughly closed my fingers around it. "I'm not asking. You will throw the ax at Jaime or you will throw it at your own target."

He stalked down to the second target and roughly pulled off the bag. Victor shook his head back and squinted in the sudden light. Other than being bound, he looked okay. The ax hung limply at my side. His eyes met mine and my anger flared. I chucked the ax at Erik. Miraculously, he caught it mid-air as he walked back toward me. He half spun and released it toward Victor.

"No!" I screamed.

The blade buried itself in his upper thigh. He didn't cry out, just looked away with a grimace. Erik kept advancing on me and I stumbled backward. He grabbed my upper arm and pulled me back to standing.

"If you are to rule, you must follow through with the hard decisions." He thrust the last ax into my hand. "Now choose."

Tears of frustration poured down my face. Jaime had almost passed out. Victor stared straight ahead, devoid of emotion. The handle began to slip from my grip as my body numbed. Erik's fingers tightened around mine, wood biting into my palm, and my knuckle popped under his grip.

"Choose," was his harsh whisper.

I took a shaky breath and took up position in front of Jaime's target. Her head lolled to the side in agony. My body lined up the shot and I prayed my aim would be true and merciful. After I swiped my eyes to remove the moisture of unshed tears, I let out a breath as the ax flew from my fingertips.

The blade sunk into the side of her skull and she went motionless. Erik walked over to Jaime's limp body, pulled one of the axes from the board and swung hard. Her head hit the ground with a wet thunk and my knees gave out. He gathered all four axes and pulled me once again to my feet.

"Don't give up yet. The game has just started." Erik laughed.

Bile rose in my throat and I searched in vain for anything that would help. Erik lined us up in front of my target and prepared to throw. My hand reached up and gently took his arm.

"No more games, Erik. You've won." He regarded me coolly but did not lower his arm. "Don't hurt my clan anymore and I'll do whatever you want."

The calm in my voice shocked even me. Erik's eyes searched my face for lies but I had none. This was beyond my desire to protect my family. The world needed this man gone and the only way to ensure that was if I did it myself. That would only happen if he let his guard down.

When he nodded, I lowered my hand and let out the breath I'd been holding. Eric's ax sailed through the air and I screamed. The blade landed inches from the left side of Victor's head. My hand twitched toward the others sitting on the stump but knew now wasn't my time.

Erik turned his back to the targets and put his arm around my waist, pulling me to his side. "How about that coffee?"

Chapter Twenty-One

E rik made terrible coffee but I swallowed the black sludge without complaint. Numbness spread through my body as I pushed every emotion down into a hole and locked them away. I'd need some serious therapy when this was over.

He talked and talked. Holy crap, this man loved the sound of his own voice. Apparently, one moment was all it took for him to trust me. That or he'd just showed me what would happen should I betray him and that should have been enough to scare me into following him down into the depths of Hell. Either way, plans and secrets were flowing.

My original guess that Erik was old was an understatement. He'd worked on a deep-sea fishing vessel and in several mines, fought in wars, some I'd never even heard of, and in his free time studied chemistry, physics, and most recently genetics. Along his way, he'd fathered many children. The last four were just this past century or so. None of the others had been living immortals or worth saving. His words, not mine.

When he finally took a breath, I asked, "You said there was another living immortal that wasn't involved in all this. Who is he?"

Erik refilled my cup. "My father. He lived a long mortal life, over seventy years, and has retired to Northern Ireland where he lives alone. The Immortal Council was only an idea when he went into seclusion. He deserves his rest."

That was *old*. The records the Council had sent me had items dating back to the eleventh century. I took another sip of coffee to cover how uncomfortable I was with all this. The resulting gag reminded me of my many mistakes.

Since we were now best pals, I risked another question. "Any chance I could have my phone back?" His dark look said everything. "Could I at least go home and get a change of clothes?"

"Dona already left to gather some of your and your sister's belongings. We'll be leaving for the Council soon so I'd rather you not wander too far."

I sent a prayer that Rowan and Eve were already gone. Rowan would fight Dona no matter what she said at this point just to know where I was. Fingers crossed, I'd also have a clean pair of underwear for this journey.

Feeling bold, I asked the question I wanted to know since he started talking hours ago. "What is the plan, exactly?"

Erik got to his feet and offered his hand. I politely refused and stood on my own, wincing at the twinge in my shoulder. Throwing axes was a great upper body workout. He didn't look upset that I'd ignored his offer when he motioned for me to follow him. Just because I was pretending to be on-board didn't mean I wasn't still my independent self. Too much submission would be a dead giveaway that I was playing him.

We passed what I thought was Acacia's room and considered stopping to check on her but I needed to follow through before Erik decided not to share all his secrets. We went down another level of steps and entered a large unfinished space.

The ceiling and walls were studs but had functional outlets; the floors were bare concrete. Long folding tables had been set up in the center under fluorescent shop lights. Five men and two women appeared to be working on various stages of something. Chemicals bubbled in one corner and someone was soldering in another. The burning metal scent made me stifle a sneeze. Six large wooden crates were lined up against the back wall.

Erik led me to one of the tables and picked up a glass cylinder, two liquids sloshed inside kept apart by a thin glass divider. Wires had been inserted into the glass connecting the two ends of the glass separation. My eyes wandered down the table and I counted twenty more.

"Phoenix Fire." He chuckled. "My own design but I couldn't come up with a better name, as this will be what will transform us from the ashes of the Immortal Council's reign. It burns hot enough to melt steel. Water speeds up the reaction so normal emergency procedures don't work."

A woman came over and carefully picked up one of the glass cylinders and carried it to her area. She lay it carefully inside a metal base and tightened four padded, plastic screws to hold it in place. Once complete, another man did a quick inspection and placed the entire assembly into one of the crates.

"You're going to blow them up?" I asked as I watched the two liquids dance inside the glass chamber.

Erik placed it back on the table and put his hands on his hips. "We're going to burn them alive then we will rise from the ashes to take our rightful place."

The faces of the Immortal Council members flashed in my mind. Some of them had only been in their positions a few months. Rowan had told me fire would kill an immortal but it took a long time. I knew from experience that living immortals still felt pain. This was once again about showing strength.

I swallowed my fear and repulsion, stuffing them down with the rest of my emotions. "When do we leave?"

He smiled at my apparent eagerness and gestured for us to go back upstairs. I followed and attempted to keep a neutral expression as if we were talking about lunch instead of mass murder. When we neared Acacia's room, he finally spoke.

"We leave tomorrow just before dusk." He hesitated before continuing, "Acacia will be fine to travel during the day, but your other clan member currently cannot."

Hope swelled within me. "We're leaving Victor here?"

Erik scratched his beard as if trying to find the correct words and my hope slowly died. "He's our guest of honor but he's been *difficult*.

You need to convince him to follow your lead and you'll need to let him have your blood."

That meant I would be able to see him to explain what was going on. Hopefully, I'd earned enough trust to do so without supervision. Dona and I would need to modify our plan slightly but we could still make it work. This was good. My expression must have changed because Erik frowned and he backed me up against the wall.

"He can have your blood because I'm allowing it. We need him to be able to travel with us during the day, without stopping. He does not get to have anything else." His eyes moved up and down my frame and I remembered the rest of his plan. "You need to start accepting your place, which is beside me. Understand?"

If I was going to make this work, he needed to believe me. Instead of pressing my back against the wall like a frightened rabbit, I leaned in. My right hand pressed against his chest. It felt like a rock wall but I gripped his shirt in my fist then pulled him in for a kiss. Bile rose in my throat but I made it as real as I could.

He kissed about as well as he made coffee. This would be the one and only time this happened. His hands wrapped around my back but I pulled away before he could go any further. The satisfied smirk on his face told me my ruse had worked.

I moved around him and reached for Acacia's doorknob before I turned back with the best smile I could fake. He nodded and headed back downstairs. Once the door was closed behind me, I ran into the attached bathroom and threw up.

• • • •

ACACIA WAS BETTER TONIGHT but even more worried about Eve. Dona showed up about an hour later with a couple changes of clothes and other assorted items she knew we would need. I grabbed my toothbrush and scrubbed until my gums bled.

"The house was empty. Rowan's car wasn't in the garage," Dona explained once I'd emerged from the bathroom.

I looked at Acacia. "I asked him to take Eve somewhere safe until this blows over."

Dona pulled a cable out of her purse and handed it to my sister. "Go ahead and charge your phone but keep it on silent. I'll make an excuse to stop by later to pick up the charger. Don't let anyone see it, okay?"

"We need to reevaluate our plan," I started but she glanced at her phone when it vibrated. "What?"

"That was my instruction to take you to go see Victor. We don't have time to talk now or you won't have enough time to do what you need."

Acacia cut in, "What's she talking about?"

I sat back down on the bed with her. "We're leaving tomorrow to meet with the Immortal Council. You'll be fine in the sunshine; Victor won't, at least not without my blood. He's also hurt." She tried to interrupt but I pressed on. "It's okay. I'll keep you safe."

Dona nodded. "We'll have time to talk later but we need to go. I'll bring her up to speed."

I gave my sister one more hug. "I'll be back soon. Once your phone works, let Eve know we're okay."

Dona hurried us to the other side of the house and down another set of stairs. Now it made sense how they got me so lost the first day. Not many places had multiple basement stairwells but then again, these weren't normal houses.

She unlocked three thick padlocks and pushed the door inward. Before I went in, she handed another duffle and a blood bag to me. "For his leg."

I nodded and stepped inside. The room looked like a carbon copy of Acacia's with different colored walls and bedsheets. Locks snapping closed gave me claustrophobia like I'd never had before. She hadn't told me when she'd be back but from her rushed movements, I doubted it was as long as I wanted.

Water was running in the attached bathroom. Victor sat on the countertop with his injured leg over the sink. Blood was everywhere. He had a sewing needle and what looked like thread from his destroyed pants in one hand. Agony clouded his features. He was attempting to sew up his own leg.

I rushed over and stilled his hands. He stared at me like I was an illusion but my eyes dropped to his injury. If he'd been a normal human, he'd have bled to death a long time ago. The gash was deep and looked to have severed an artery. I wasn't sure if the amount of blood Dona gave me was going to be enough considering it had been a while since he'd had any at all.

When he noticed that I held the bag, he snatched it away and tore the corner open. I looked away. Everything about this situation was wrong. Once the empty bag hit the floor, I turned back. He was standing but still leaning on the counter for support. The gash was now an angry red mark, muscle looked connected but distorted. It hadn't been enough.

I helped him wash the blood off his hands and leg before helping him back to the bedroom. We collapsed on the bed and I let out a breath as I lay on my back next to him.

"I'm sorry." His voice was quiet.

"Stop apologizing," I grumbled and sat upright, staring straight ahead. "We don't have time to feel sorry for ourselves right now."

His hand found mine and I closed my eyes. "I told you I'd keep Acacia safe but they separated us immediately. That poison they gave you doesn't kill reborn but it does incapacitate them by burning off their blood reserves."

I turned back to face him. "She's fine. Well, as fine as to be expected. Time is running out and I need to bring you up to speed."

His hand lifted, threading into my hair, and cupped the side of my face. It was clear, he wasn't okay either. Fuck. I needed him to focus. When he pulled me in for the kiss, I didn't resist. Then, it was me who needed to focus.

His lips moved from mine down my neck, scrambling my brain. "We're, um, leaving tomorrow. You need to take my blood because of the sun."

Words were way too hard right now and the thought crossed my mind that this may be the last time we would be together. Regardless of if I succeeded or failed tomorrow, my life would be over.

His teeth broke the skin and emotions threatened to drown me. Everything I'd been shoving down to make this work crashed around me in waves. Tears leaked from the corners of my eyes and passion fogged my thoughts. I didn't want to die but I didn't see any other choice. If this was to be my last night, I'd spend it how I wanted.

Once he lifted his head to kiss me again, I gently pressed him down on the bed. My lips traced a similar path down this throat. I'd need his power of persuasion if my plan was to work. Erik hadn't explicitly told me not to take Victor's blood so he couldn't punish me. Plus, I needed to heal. His strength would return once Dona got him more blood and my need was too important for the plan.

Hands and lips wandered, becoming less and less gentle. At some point, all our clothing was shed. Either my blood or the euphoria gave him strength because he flipped me over onto my back and buried himself inside me. I wrapped my legs around him and increased the rhythm.

"Tell me you love me," I whispered, realizing he'd never said the words out loud.

He locked eyes with me. "I love you, Arabella. You are everything. The reason I exist. There is nothing in this world I won't do to prove that."

The honesty of his words broke me. I reached up and pulled him in for a kiss. Another tear escaped and I had to hold back a sob. I really wanted to be loved for who I was, not who someone wanted me to be. After everything I'd been through, I fucking deserved it.

My orgasm surprised me and I had to bite my cheek to keep from screaming. He came a moment later. We both lay still, just holding onto the moment. The realization of what I could have and knowing I was going to lose it so soon made my breathing hitch. Victor misunderstood my reaction and pulled me closer, kissing the side of my face.

I let myself lay there for another few minutes then got up and went to the bathroom to get dressed. Some cold water on my face and a quick finger comb through my hair was enough to recenter myself. Love was never in my future. I needed to stop thinking otherwise.

When I stepped back into the bedroom, Victor was sitting up waiting for me but I spoke first. "We're leaving tomorrow at dusk. You need to follow my lead without question. Can you do that for me?"

A spark of the old Victor shone through. "And if I don't?"

"Then we're both as good as dead. You swore your allegiance to me. Now you get to prove it."

His eyes searched my face as I heard a key enter the first lock. We'd run out of time and we both knew it. I should say the words back to him. He deserved it too. If it meant he'd listen to me tomorrow, I'd say it even if I wasn't sure it was true yet. I stuffed my emotions back into the hole and rushed over to give him one more kiss.

"I love you too," I whispered against his lips then pushed passed Dona into the hallway.

Chapter Twenty-Two

Dona and I hurried back to Acacia's room so I could share the finalized plan with them. Neither were happy but they couldn't offer an alternative. Everyone agreed Erik needed to be stopped and this might be our only chance. Dona would bring Tyson up to speed and get me what I needed before we left tonight. She mentioned there were a few others that would back us up if needed too.

It was almost dawn when we parted ways. Dona left me with a notepad to write my goodbyes and the promise they would be delivered. I stared at the blank page for over an hour before I finally laid down next to my sister. Leaving her was hurting me the most. Rowan would make sure everyone was taken care of and she'd always have Eve. My parents knew how much I loved them and my fierce desire to protect the ones I love. They'd understand. In the end, no words were needed so the pages would stay blank forever.

I made it clear that no one was to tell Victor my plan. He had to go along as if nothing had changed. In the depths of my heart, I knew he'd try to stop me, tell me that I was being emotional instead of rational. When dealing with a narcissistic maniac like Erik, emotions were the only thing that would get us through this.

Try as I might, my brain wouldn't slow down enough to sleep. After tossing and turning for what felt like hours, I got up and took a shower then sorted through the few items Dona brought in the duffle bags. Clothes and a few toiletries. Either she had been rushed or the bag had been searched before she was allowed to give it to me. I guessed the latter.

We'd be traveling in a three-vehicle caravan and weren't coming back to this house after the trip to the Council. Two would carry the Phoenix Fire and the other would be full of Erik's entourage and all our belongings. Dona wasn't entirely sure where we were headed after the

Council meeting. Apparently, Erik only trusted her so much or maybe he hadn't planned that far yet.

There was a knock on the door late afternoon. Dona poked her head in followed by a tray of food. My stomach growled but I didn't feel hungry.

Her voice was low when she spoke. "Everyone is set. Tyson's switched the triggers so the one Erik's holding will be useless. Yours is under the plate. Hide it and make sure you are ready before you press the button. There won't be a delay."

She put the tray down and wrapped me in a hug. I returned the gesture of affection; her earlier betrayal long forgiven. If anyone understood loyalty to family, it was me. I'd never fully appreciated all she'd done for me and now it was too late.

"Make sure Acacia rides with you. Whatever excuse you need to make, keep her close. She can't be in the same car as Erik and me."

"Already done. Erik asked me to organize the vehicles. You'll be riding with Erik, Tyson, and Victor in one of the vans with Phoenix Fire. Michael will be driving. He's loyal to Erik and will be collateral damage but won't be missed."

"Can't you get Victor into another car?"

She shook her head. "Erik insisted on that one. He wanted to be able to keep an eye on you both during the trip."

Of course he did. At least I had Victor's power of persuasion. It was the only trick I had up my sleeve, other than the trigger that is. One more wrinkle to my almost perfect plan.

"Tell Tyson to get Victor out of the car at my signal by whatever means necessary. I won't lose any more of my people in this war."

She searched my face. "Are you sure there isn't another way?"

I shook my head and embraced her once more. She left and I ate whatever she brought without tasting it but needing the energy to get through this. Activity could be heard through the door as the afternoon ticked by. I attempted to nap but never fell asleep for more than a few minutes, leaving me with nothing but a headache and a bad mood.

There was no knock when Erik strode into the room. He looked positively jovial seeing his plan nearly coming to fruition. He wore a new age rock shirt and I wondered if he had actually listened to the band. They were awful.

"Ready to save the world?" he asked.

"You have no idea." The words fell from my lips before I thought them through but not understanding the context made him grin.

"Walk with me. Dona will collect the bags and your sister shortly."

I followed him to the main part of the house. He handed me a cup of coffee and as tired as I was, I knew it would just make me feel sick so I only pretended to sip on it.

"Once the Council's strings have been snipped, you'll feel better. We really do want the same thing, Arabella."

He led us outside and I took a deep breath. This was my world. I'd never lived outside of this town and never wanted to. I loved the smell of the air, the change of the seasons, and all the wonderful memories I'd made here. Erik watched me with fascination.

"We could come back to this area once the war is over. This seems like a nice place to raise a family." My expression faltered before I could help it and he laughed. "No rush on that. War is no place for children."

The three white panel vans sat in a row at the end of the drive. Watching the final crate being loaded and secured made this very real. Dona appeared shortly after with armloads of bags to put into another vehicle. She played her part perfectly by keeping focused on her instructions and ignoring me. The trigger felt heavy in the pocket of my jacket, my fingers wrapped around it like a lifeline.

"Where are we going after?" I asked and tilted my cup to my lips to fake a drink.

"Nevada." Erik watched the progress and people milling about. "We've secured a house from the Council until we can rise from the proverbial ashes so to speak. Sam's gone ahead to get us set up."

The mention of this son made me think of Jaime. How had Sam reacted when he learned of her punishment, of her death? They seemed to genuinely care about each other but then again, it may have just been a ruse to make me comfortable around them. Erik must have faith in him and his mindset to send him ahead to the start on the next phase of the plan.

The man who had brought out Jaime for her punishment approached. "We're all set."

"Thanks, Michael. Go ahead and get everyone in their assigned spots. Time to take this show on the road."

While he was speaking, I dumped the coffee onto the ground. "Can I use the bathroom before we go?"

Erik nodded his head toward the house and I hurried back inside. Once in the kitchen half bath, I pushed the button lock then sat on the toilet with my head between my knees. Closing my eyes and taking a few deep breaths helped. The plan was sound. I could do this.

I had to do this for my clan and all the other clans about to be dragged into this senseless war. After one more look in the mirror, I let out a slow breath and walked outside toward my death.

• • • •

MICHAEL AND ERIK SAT in the front of the first van. Victor sat behind Erik. I was squished in the middle of the small bench seat with Tyson behind the driver. I was too tall for this shit but the men on either side of me were taller so it made sense. Plus, Erik could keep an eye on me with little effort on his part. The third row of seats had been removed to make room for the four large Phoenix fire crates.

Our middle seats had rolling doors on each side so Tyson and Victor could easily get out on my signal. It would've been easier if the guys were sitting together but I couldn't risk alerting Erik by asking to move. I'd physically kick Victor out if I had to. His hands were bound in front of him so he would be off balance but he would survive a fall from a moving vehicle.

Dona was driving the van behind us with Acacia and a handful of others I didn't know. The last van held a single driver and eight more crates. When the vehicle started to roll forward, I had to slow my breathing to calm down. I moved my foot so it rested against Victor's as if to pull strength from him. His knee shifted so it touched my leg. This would hurt him so much.

The caravan moved slowly through town and I craned my neck to get one last glimpse at some of my favorite places. What looked like my dad's truck passed us and I shut my eyes to center myself. Erik turned around to look at me and I shifted my leg away from Victor's.

"Are you okay?" Erik asked.

"Carsick. Can I switch seats with Tyson in case I need to throw up?"

He opened the glove box and tossed me a tiny bottle. "I wish you'd mentioned it earlier. We aren't stopping."

To keep up the ruse, I popped one of the pills and handed the bottle back. Victor gave me a questioning look. He knew I didn't have car sickness. From his expression, he also knew I was up to something but thankfully held his tongue.

Dona was supposed to fall behind at a stoplight as we neared the on-ramp. I glanced in the rearview mirror to see her and the other van still right behind us. There was only one more light before we got on the interstate. What was she waiting for?

The stoplight ahead of us turned yellow and I expected the van to speed through it but it slowed to a stop, keeping all three vans packed together. Clearly, the dangerous cargo was making the driver overly cautious and also ruining my plan. When the light turned green, we rolled forward but Dona's van stayed still. Erik noticed in the side mirror and began to turn.

Victor raised his bound hands to my face and kissed me hard. So many emotions burned through me but the distraction worked. Erik fully turned in his seat to break us up. His attention focused on Victor, not the vans falling behind.

"I love you." Victor's voice was almost too low for me to hear, then louder he said, "Now."

Two things happened at once. Michael put his foot to the floor and the van shot forward, throwing Erik off balance. Tyson wrenched open the door on his side, wrapped his arms around my waist, and pulled us both out. We flew out the door as the van continued to pick up speed on the on-ramp. Grit burned into the side of my arm and face as we slid along the concrete. An oncoming car honked and served to avoid us.

As soon as we stopped sliding, I elbowed Tyson in the gut and jumped to my feet, running after the van. This was not the plan! We weren't going to get another chance like this. Victor needed to get out so I could push the trigger. My hand found nothing but an empty pocket and I stumbled in realization.

A fiery explosion knocked me off my feet and back the way I'd come. The air was so hot it scorched my lungs, driving out my breath in a rush of pain. The back of my head smacked against the concrete and my ears stopped working except for a high-pitched squeal. I rolled to my side and watched the horror.

The force of the blast peeled the top of the van forward like a tuna can, which was still rolling slowly forward. White-blue flames encased the entire vehicle. A second explosion added red flames and a pillar of black smoke to the wreckage.

I screamed with no sound. My heart felt like it was the one covered in Phoenix Fire. It was supposed to be me! No one else was supposed to get hurt. Someone grabbed my shoulders and attempted to help me to my feet. I fought them and tried to move closer to the flames. Maybe I could still save him.

Tyson shook me and spoke but I couldn't hear him. He said it again slower so I could read his lips.

"We need to go."

I shook my head and sagged in his grip. "No! I'm not leaving him!"

Suddenly, Dona and Acacia were pushing me toward the other van. I wasn't strong enough to resist all three and they were able to get me into the back of the van and shut the door. Dona made a U-turn and headed back the way we'd come then pulled into a residential area where she slowed way down. I didn't know if the other van followed because I didn't care.

A tinny ringing joined the high-pitched squeal in my ears and I felt tears streaming down my face. My lungs and arm burned and my head pounded. They'd all conspired against me, using my own plan but never intending for me to be the one to push the trigger. The goal was to kill Erik and we had succeeded but the loss was too great. I was expendable. It was supposed to be me!

My body curled into a ball and I let my tears flow. Acacia crawled to me and put my head in her lap. I gripped her as if she was the only thing keeping me together. Right now, I think she was. The van drove for what felt like an eternity.

When we stopped, I reached up and touched my ear. My hand came away bloody. The force of the blast must have ruptured my ear drums. Ringing continued to block out all else. Artificial light filled my vision as the back doors were pulled open. Steve attempted to take me out of the van but I resisted.

Dona held up a piece of paper, understanding that I couldn't hear. *You couldn't be involved. Go inside so I can go back and make sure it is done.*

"Save him," I demanded with no sound.

She looked at Tyson then back to me and nodded. There was nothing either of them could do but I had to try. I'd worded it as a demand. She'd have to do everything in her power to follow my request. It was selfish and unrealistic but I couldn't help it. My selfishness could cost her life too but I was too far gone to take it back.

My legs refused to hold me upright once the fight left my body. Steve gently removed me from the van and carried me up to my rooms. He laid me on the bed but I immediately tried to get up again. Acacia started speaking but I shook my head and pointed to my ears in frustration.

She opened my nightstand and pulled out my journal and pen. *Let me help you.*

I didn't deserve it so I shook my head as fresh tears blurred my vision. She punched me in the arm and pushed the paper in my direction again. Time wouldn't heal my physical wounds, not anymore. Nothing would ever heal my emotional ones. After another push from my sister, I nodded and took her blood.

Once the ringing was reduced to a tolerable level, I pulled my pillow to my chest and folded myself back into a protective ball. "It was supposed to be me."

Acacia laid down and put her arm around me. "It was never going to be you. Victor planned on this from the day we arrived at Erik's. He'd bragged about the Phoenix Fire the entire drive to the house. We lied when we told you they separated us right away. Victor knew his life was forfeit and wanted to end it his way, not the Council's."

I broke into tears again, fingers tightening around the pillowcase so tight it hurt. Everything I'd suppressed since I found out I was a living immortal came out. My shoulders and chest ached from the weight of it all leaving my body. I never wanted any of this. Dying today was the one thing that I could control, that had been my decision. Damn him for taking that away from me. Damn him for leaving me alone.

Chapter Twenty-Three

I slept through an entire day and couldn't face anyone the next. Rowan had come in at some point but I wasn't ready to talk so I pretended to be asleep. He didn't buy it for a second and told me Dona had come back alone. He sounded as destroyed as I felt. The sobbing started again and he sat beside me with his hand on my back until I fell asleep. A bottle of water and a protein bar were on my nightstand when I woke up later.

The third day, I finally crawled out of bed and stood in the shower. Shivers wracked my body as I forgot to turn on the water for a full five minutes. The temperature had plummeted outside as the early Fall rains began. It was like nature had changed to match my mood.

It was midafternoon when I finally emerged from my room. All was quiet and I let out a sigh of relief. I needed a few minutes to walk the house alone. My tears had dried up and I had a new mission.

Just one more stop before I could move forward.

The walk down to the third basement level took a lifetime because I'd stopped and turned multiple times before finally making it to my destination. My hand shook as I reached for Victor's door. I'd come to say goodbye the only way I knew how. The room looked exactly the same. Clearly, no one else had come in yet.

My fingers trailed along his desk and rested momentarily on his closed laptop, warm from charging. I gripped the back of the leather recliner as my eyes slowly scanned his bedroom. The satiny-soft sheets were rumpled from sleep and the duvet was barely holding onto one bottom corner. My eyes burned but I had nothing left to give.

Finally gathering courage, I sat on the bed and hugged a pillow to my chest. Victor's scent enveloped me and for a moment, I felt like if I opened my eyes he'd be standing in front of me. He'd apologize for giving us all a scare and promise to never leave my side again. Time seemed to slow as I held onto the stupid pillow like my life depended on it. No one magically appeared and the room stayed painfully silent.

When my arms ached from the death grip I'd had on the pillow, I went to the closet and pulled out two garment bags, checking to make sure they contained what I wanted. I'd need help moving the record player but that could wait. In the bathroom, a bottle of cologne sat on the vanity. I lifted the cap and let the scent wash over me, trying to remember how it used to make me nervous. The only memory I could conjure was our last.

"I think I could've loved you but you didn't give me a chance." My voice sounded hollow, like it wasn't really me speaking. "We were supposed to have all the time in the world. I'll make sure your sacrifice was worth it."

With the garment bags slung over my arm and the bottle of cologne in my other hand, I shut the door behind me. That door and my heart would stay closed forever. I vowed at that moment to never enter these rooms again.

Dona found me several hours later in the office. I'd made a cup of coffee but it sat untouched as I typed furiously on the laptop. Hours had flown by as I put together my new plan.

"Arabella?" she asked timidly.

"I need you to get me the list of all the living immortals that agreed to fight with Erik." When she didn't respond, I looked up. "Once I have that, schedule a meeting with Councilwoman Tsu."

I picked up my mug and walked toward her. Her large glasses and contacts were gone. She could once again be who she wanted, even her clothes looked more comfortable. This was what I was fighting for now. Real freedom, not Erik's bullshit version.

"I did everything I could," she said in a broken whisper.

Her words made my throat tighten. There was nothing that could be done. Erik had designed the Phoenix Fire to be resistant to standard fire suppression, only increasing the strength of the blaze. As soon as that trigger was pressed, everyone in that car was gone. All I could hope for was that Victor hadn't suffered.

My hand rested on her shoulder. "I know. Thank you."

Arguing sounded from the kitchen but I didn't have enough strength to care. Tyson and Steve were postured up and yelling at each other about who knew what. I stepped around them and dumped the cold coffee for a hot refill. At my appearance, they both relaxed and stopped fighting.

Once the new pot was brewing, I walked over to Steve and put my arms around his waist and rested my head against his chest. After a moment, he returned the favor and we just stood in silence. He'd been unconscious but I knew he would blame himself for not being able to protect all of us.

"I'm glad you're okay," I said.

He chuckled. "I'm tougher than I look."

I laughed and stepped back, turning to Tyson. "Thank you for saving me. You can stay as long as you'd like." Steve started to interrupt so I held up my hand. "This is my clan. If he wants to stay, he can. It's not my job to make everyone happy. If you want happy, go talk to Eve."

They glared at each other and Steve finally broke eye contact and stomped outside. I let out a deep breath and finished prepping my coffee. Theirs was a problem that would be dealt with in time.

"Sam's gone," Tyson said from behind me.

"Is that going to be a problem?" I asked, adding another spoonful of sugar into my steaming mug.

"I don't know, but I don't think so. At least not now." I made eye contact with him. "He truly loved Jaime. Magnus, I mean Erik, sent him ahead because he didn't trust his state of mind. The hurt was too fresh. My father wasn't sure if he'd sabotage the Council attack as a type of revenge for his loss. Sam will probably shift the blame at some point since our father is gone."

I nodded in understanding. There was a chance he'd eventually blame me for her death but that was a battle for another day. Right now, he needed to get away from his feelings of loss and his father's madness. Seems like Victor had saved more than just me.

"You'll be safe here. Steve knows how to follow orders. If I tell him you're part of the clan, then you are," I said, taking a sip and letting the warm richness relax my entire being. "Let me know if you'd like to make it official but I'm good either way."

His forehead creased in confusion but he seemed like a smart guy. He'd figure it out. Especially after my meeting with Tsu. I had been honest with Erik when I told him that I was on-board with this plan, just not his methods. The Immortal Council seemed to have overlooked the fact that they were supposed to be supporting and protecting *all* immortals, not just living ones. They wanted me to have a platform. Too bad they weren't going to be able to veto this one. That's why I needed that list from Dona.

The printer was going when I walked back into the office. We'd need to modify the space so we could both comfortably work in here. I'd get Acacia involved. She was good at space planning. This mission was going to take time and for once it *was* on our side.

"Here's the list." She handed the double-sided sheet to me and I glanced at a few of the names. One in particular jumped out at me.

"Did you schedule the meeting?"

She nodded. "Tomorrow night at eleven. You have an email with a HIPAA subject line. I left it open for you."

From her expression, she'd read it. Only Rowan knew about this and now Dona. Soon, it would be on record with the Council. It was the one last small thing I could do for Victor.

• • • •

"COUNCILWOMAN TSU. IT'S nice to see you," I said as she popped up on my computer screen.

I could hear people murmuring in the background. She appeared to be sitting in a conference room, books lined the wall behind her. Tsu's expression was pinched. Clearly, she didn't like being summoned—especially for an unknown reason.

"We don't usually like to meet in this format but your assistant said it was urgent."

I straightened in my seat. "Several urgent matters actually. First of which is to inform you that the rogue issue has been resolved. Erik Magnus is dead."

The voices in the background rose and she motioned for them to quiet. "Are you certain?"

Somehow, I'd always known they had more on him than they provided me and I was tired of being left in the dark. "Yes. I've cleaned up one of your messes and now you owe me one."

Tsu brushed an imaginary bit of lint off her blouse. "That's not how the Immortal Council works."

"Is Gutierrez present?" I asked. A moment later, his head was visible behind hers and he gave me a little wave. "Did you get my email with the attachment?"

"Just now," he replied.

"Open it so the rest of the Council can read it. I'd like it added to my formal records."

There was a moment's pause and the sound of typing. Everyone glanced over the screen at what I guessed was some sort of projector. I waited as they read the file.

"I don't understand how this is pressing." Tsu finally met my eyes.

"Because you sentenced an innocent man. Victor was convicted with the murder of my first child. As you can see, that wasn't the case. I need you to reverse the sentence effectively immediately."

Tsu looked uncomfortable. "We've been given notice that Mr. River is no longer with us."

"And this matters because?" My temper was rising and I had to take a deep breath to keep the malice from my voice. "He didn't shoot me. He didn't kill my child. His only crime was loving me. Reverse the sentence."

She held my gaze for several seconds then nodded. I heard more typing. "It is done. Was that all you wanted to discuss?"

I took another deep breath and let it out. This would either start a war or start us on a better path for the future. Either way, I wasn't backing down. My clan deserved this and so did I.

"I will not be needing the rest of the extension to declare my platform. I've made my decision and you will not be vetoing this one." Her questioning look turned worried when I took time to sip my coffee. "Immortal Council Reform. Gutierrez has received a signed petition from all the living immortals ready to make this happen. Either you will work with us or against us."

She sputtered and her eyes jumped above the camera again. I assumed he'd put the list up on the projector. He was the first person I'd spoken to about the reform and he was also willing to be the only one in the room who had signed it when the list was announced.

"This is outrageous! This is not how things are done!" Tsu spat.

"It is now." I leaned forward. "Either you will lose two thirds of your living immortals or you will work with us to make it a better world for both reborn and living immortals alike. You have... Five months to decide."

Throwing her words back at her felt good. Her expression told me everything I needed to know. She was scared. Sixty-seven names were on that list, including mine and Erik's father. Tyson had provided me a way to contact him. He hadn't bowed out of the fight; he'd been left out. After a very staticky phone call, I found that he was not fond of being left in the dark either.

Tsu finally quieted the rest of the attending councilmembers. She'd pressed mute and leaned out of frame so I knew they were deliberating on the spot. I tried to keep my expression neutral while I waited but my heart pounded in my chest. Win or lose, everything would change today.

Tsu unmuted herself and straightened her blouse. "How do you propose we start?"

I smiled and sat back. "I've got a few ideas. Are you ready?"

Epilogue – Three Years Later

The warm Spring day was coming to a close. A breeze stirred the trees as the sky began to change colors. I adjusted myself to push the long swing bench in the newly completed gazebo situated alongside the house. It had taken Steve a bit longer than planned to finish it. Mostly because he started over several times until he got it just right. Fairy lights adorned the ceiling and down the sides so it could be used day and night. It was one of my favorite places in the world.

He and Tyson were heading out for the evening soon. Considering how they'd fought like little old ladies when Tyson first arrived, everyone was shocked when they announced they were seeing each other. They'd moved in together in one of the large suites last week and I couldn't be happier for them. Three years had gone by in a flash. I absentmindedly rubbed the pearl in my necklace between my fingers.

The Immortal Council wasn't entirely disbanded but it had been completely revamped. Pun one hundred percent intended. The Council, as it was now called, consisted of five people. Two living immortals and three reborn. Seats were awarded by nomination from the previous seat holders every four years or would be once we got that far. Right now, Tsu and Guiterrez held the two living immortal spots, Joseph held one of the reborn. I had met the other two and they seemed capable enough but their names weren't important to me.

I'd been asked to sit in on hundreds of meetings as the entire system was being restructured. Luckily, I was able to do most of it remotely. The biggest change was after their first year of transition, reborns could live without being bound to a living immortal if they chose to. They still needed to follow the guidelines of the Council since mortal laws didn't really cover everything related to being immortal, but in the end, almost everyone stayed attached to a living immortal. For the few who had left, only a handful hadn't been able to handle life on their own. All of my clan had stayed with me, except one, and I'd gained a few lost souls along the way, some only temporarily as they navigated into this new world.

The crunch of tires slowly made their way down the long driveway so I sent a quick text. *Eve, your ride's here.*

I heard the car stop and the door open then close. My back was to the driveway as I was watching something more important. Threats were a thing of the past, at least for now.

"Daddy!" a tiny voice squealed and my breath caught.

I turned to see Tom walking toward us. Before she toddled too far, I scooped the little girl into my arms and walked in his direction, giving her belly a tickle. Giggles filled the air and I smiled but he'd frozen in place at her words.

When we were close, I spoke to her. "No Victoria, this isn't Daddy. This is your Uncle Tom."

I watched as they studied each other. She was the most beautiful thing in my world. A mess of dark curls surrounded her chubby face. Her eyes were something special. Thick, dark lashes surrounded light gray irises streaked with gold. There were none other like them because she was truly one of a kind.

"Hi Tom," I said after a moment of silence. "I didn't realize you were Eve's ride."

He tore his gaze from my daughter and stared at me for a moment. "I—I had no idea."

I shifted the toddler onto my hip. "We're trying to keep it quiet as long as we can. She's kind of a big deal to the immortal world."

"She's beautiful, but how could she not be." He reached over and twisted one of her curls out of her face, which she quickly pushed back with the flat of her hand.

"I'm sorry I can't make it to the wedding. Send Rachel my best. I'm really happy for you both."

"Thanks." Tom hesitated. "God, this is awkward."

"Only if you make it that way." I shook my head. "Tom, you will always be my first love and what we had was amazing. You showed me I was worthy of love but we both knew it wasn't forever, no matter how much we wanted it to be."

"Who's a stinky, stinky boy?" Eve's voice sounded from the front of the house followed by another high-pitched giggle.

When she rounded the corner, she stopped. Apparently, she hadn't known Tom was picking her up either. She recovered quickly and made her way to us, setting down the toddler in her arms. Once again, Tom was dumb struck.

"I've heard twins run in your family," I said as I put Victoria down next to her brother.

Lucas immediately reached toward Tom who leaned over and carefully picked him up. The toddler patted him gently on the face and pulled on a long strand of hair. Lucas looked like his sister but instead of the gray-gold eyes, his were brilliant blue. We didn't know why and for now it didn't matter.

"I feel so guilty. You shouldn't have to do this alone."

I laughed. "I'm never alone."

Eve tossed her hair over her shoulder. "I swear Rowan is like a creepy stalker. He's got you and the twins under constant surveillance."

I nodded in agreement. "It also helps that they have the best live-in aunt ever. Is Acacia meeting you in California?"

Eve nodded. "Yep. She's actually in San Fran right now."

"Tell her I love her?" I asked.

Acacia left once the dust settled. She wasn't mad at me anymore but she needed time to figure out who she was without me or Eve around. Rowan had met up with her a few times but I was giving her the space she needed. Her last message told me how excited she was to be part of an art exhibition in Chicago. That was around Christmas time. I had no idea she was back on the West Coast.

Tom put Lucas down when he started to squirm and the twins toddled back toward the gazebo. They loved the lights as much as I did and I knew they couldn't get too far too quickly. Besides, I'm sure Rowan was watching from somewhere.

I wrapped Eve in a hug. "Have fun and tell your mom hi for me."

"Yeah, that'll be fun." She squeezed me back. "Are you sure you guys can't come? I'm not sure I can survive a week without those little squishies."

I shook my head. She knew why I couldn't go. There were only a few who knew the twins existed or even that they were possible. Erik was gone but his ideals still buzzed in the background, quieted slightly by the changes I had worked so hard to create. Sam had disappeared and the Council had yet to find him. Dona had received a couple texts from him but always from different phone numbers so at least we knew he was still alive.

I opened my arms and gave Tom a hug too. He pulled me tight and held on a moment too long. "I wish I'd known."

I held him and let myself remember how it used to feel. "It wouldn't have mattered."

Before he let go, he whispered, "Did you love him?"

That familiar lump in my throat threatened and I pulled back, knowing that the unshed tears made my eyes shine. "What matters is I love what he gave me."

He nodded then put his arm around Eve's shoulders. They turned and walked back to the front of the house. Giggles sounded behind me. My hand went to my necklace once again. I wasn't alone and now I would never have to feel that way again.

About the Author

Melinda Call grew up in the Pacific Northwest and Mountain West of the United States. She loves her family fiercely, even the four-legged ones that don't speak clearly. Her hobbies include reading, gardening, and baking. Feeding the people she cares about is her love language. She talks too much and cries during almost every movie/TV show/commercial that she doesn't fall asleep watching. Even though she is a scientist by day, she whole-heartedly believes magic exists.

Check out Melinda's website, https://melindacall.com, to read about her crazy life, books, freebies, and for links to follow her on social media.

Make sure to sign up for her newsletter[1] so you never miss any big announcements.

---

1. https://melindacallauthor.eo.page/6c4th

Other Books by Melinda Call

Blood Target Part 1 and 2, prequel to *Blood Match*. Links for the free eBook downloads at https://www.melindacall.com.

Blood Match, Book One of the Blood Match Series. Purchase eBook or paperback at your favorite retailers.

Blood Bound, Book Two of the Blood Match Series. Purchase eBook or paperback at your favorite retailers.

www.ingramcontent.com/pod-product-compliance
Lightning Source LLC
Chambersburg PA
CBHW051658260626
47170CB00004B/1568